THE LOVE
DETECTIVE

THE LOVE
DETECTIVE

•

CAROLINE CRANE

AVALON BOOKS
THOMAS BOUREGY AND COMPANY, INC.
401 LAFAYETTE STREET
NEW YORK, NEW YORK 10003

PRINTED IN THE UNITED STATES OF AMERICA
ON ACID-FREE PAPER
BY HADDON CRAFTSMEN, SCRANTON, PENNSYLVANIA

THE LOVE
DETECTIVE

Chapter One

Lily walked more slowly, watching each house number as she approached the address on East Sixteenth Street. It was a pleasant neighborhood of brownstones and small apartment buildings, with tree-shaded sidewalks. It was a nice place to work, but it wouldn't be for long.

"A few days," the agency had told her. "Just typing and answering the phone. No word processing. It's a one-man office. A private investigator."

The building was a brownstone, four stories high, on the south side of the block. It had two entrances, one at the top of a flight of steps, the other tucked underneath like the door to a hobbit's burrow. Next to it was a sign that said BARBERINI.

1

There was no reference to a private investigator. "Barberini" could have been anything. A dress designer. A dentist. Except then it would have had some initials after it.

She paused to brush the wrinkles from her blue chambray skirt. It had been a rough subway ride. Her blouse was white and tailored, her blond hair tucked into a shining French twist. She patted it to be sure there were no loose ends, and checked her pantyhose for snags. Even with a temp job, first impressions mattered. Finally satisfied that she looked trim and professional, she rang the doorbell.

An answering buzzer released the catch. She entered a dim, gray-painted hallway that went through to the back of the building. On her right, an open door led into a spacious room, much too large for the single desk that faced her from the opposite wall.

The desk was unoccupied, which left her wondering what to do. Above her head, fluorescent lighting shone down on a faded carpet of Persian design. An oriel window faced the street, its three panels broken only by a softly blowing air conditioner.

As she took a tentative step into the room, a man entered through a door at the far corner. He was a young man, scarcely more than thirty, tall and darkly handsome. His cheekbones were high, his hair blue-black with a slight wave to it. He wore a white dress shirt open at the neck, and had taken off the jacket to his dark gray suit.

"Is this the private investigator's office?" Lily asked. "I'm Felicia Foster. I was sent by McCavity Temps."

"Good," he said. "I'm glad you're here. Can you type and answer the phone?"

"Of course I can answer the phone. And I type sixty words a minute."

"Are you responsible? I need somebody who can look after the office. I have to be out a lot."

"I consider myself responsible. Maybe this will help." She reached into her oversize purse and handed him one of her résumés. She had been carrying them with her for five months while she looked for a permanent job.

With some surprise (since most temp workers did not bring résumés) he took it and began to read.

"Twenty-four years old." And then: "Penn State?"

She smiled. It sounded as though he considered it an asset, although probably he wondered why a person with her background would be working as a temporary typist.

"Editorial assistant for *World Week*," he read further. "What made you leave a job like that?"

"The magazine stopped publishing. I was there three years."

He had probably never heard of it. *World Week* was scarcely a threat to *Time* or *Newsweek*.

He mulled over her name. "Felicia Foster. That's nice. Is it your real name?"

"Yes, but most people call me Lily. I like that better."

"Too bad," he said. "I like Felicia Foster. It has rhythm."

"And alliteration." Maybe that was what he meant. "It gets worse. I'm engaged to a man named Flynn."

"No, don't overdo it." He almost smiled. He really was good-looking, in a slick sort of way. The only flaw was a very thin scar at the right side of his mouth. "I'm Al Barberini. Just call me Al. You wouldn't be from Minnesota, would you?"

"New Jersey. I live in Manhattan now."

"You have that cool, blond northern look. Swedish, or something. Okay, this is where you're stationed." He patted the back of the desk chair. "Your job is looking after people, answering the phone, taking care of clients. Usually the phone gets pretty busy. It's behaving right now."

She supposed the desk had a surface, but it was buried under files, phone books, African violets, and a transcribing machine. A rolling table next to it held an IBM typewriter. She sat down, then stood up again and lowered the chair.

He watched her sadly, rubbing his chin. "She was shorter than you. A little package of dynamite, really kept the place going. But just last night . . . " He flicked his fingers. "Poof!"

"Your secretary? She didn't give you any notice?"

He shrugged. "It's not easy in the middle of a stroke."

Lily gasped. "A stroke? How old was she?"

"Seventy-seven. There are worse ways to go."

"How come she was still working at seventy-seven?"

"That's the way she wanted it." A scowl flickered across his slender eyebrows, as though Lily had accused him of slave labor. "And she was good. I'm going to have a hard time replacing her. There's an ad running in the paper, so you might get calls from applicants. Tell them to send in their bio. I rented a P.O. box for that." He wrote down the number for her. "Don't give out the street address. I want to do some screening before I see anybody."

Lily could sympathize with the applicants. "I always hate it when I have to write to a P.O. box. It takes so long. And they never call. I'd rather confront people directly."

"I don't want to be confronted directly," he explained. "A P.I. attracts too many crazies. How long have you been temping?"

"Five months. I'm looking, but it's hard when you don't know how to do word processing. I want something that pays decently and isn't just donkey work. My roommates tell me I'm too picky. My boyfriend thinks I'm not picky enough. He liked that magazine job. Editorial assistant sounds better than it is."

"So," he said, "everybody has an opinion. What about you?"

The last time she confided her dream was to Donald Flynn. He had laughed at her. But this man would be in and out of her life in a twinkling. What he thought didn't matter.

"I want to earn enough so I can go to law school. I want to do something worthwhile with my life."

"Is your boyfriend a lawyer?" he asked.

"He's in medical school. One year to go. That's why I moved to the city. I could have stayed with my folks in Oradell, but I wanted to be near Donald."

The phone rang. He answered it and gave his post office box address to a job applicant.

"I have some calls to make," he told Lily. "I'll be on line three. The other two are yours. You know how to do that, don't you?"

Assured that she could operate a push-button telephone, he retired to his own office. It was the last of three rooms strung in a row like railroad cars. Lily could see straight through them to a window that looked out onto greenery—a city garden. She could see Al at his desk, talking endlessly on the phone.

It rang again. She could not remember how he had answered. "Mr. Barberini's office," she said.

"Is he there?" barked a voice.

"He's on the phone right now. Could I have him call you?"

"I'll get back." The voice hung up.

She wrote Al a note, asking if he wanted to be interrupted, and took it to him.

It gave her a chance to see the rest of the suite. The middle room, the smallest, was kept as a utility area. It had two empty desks, one with a fax machine on it. There were a copier, a supply cabinet, and numerous file boxes.

Al's office had rays of sunlight coming through its two south windows. The greenery she had seen was mostly ivy. A London plane tree grew between concrete slabs, and a box of pink geraniums sat on a ledge against the wall.

He had the phone loosely to his ear and was pecking at a computer. She handed him her note.

He shook his head. ''Don't put anybody through. I'm busy.'' Feeling the need to explain his current idleness, he added, ''I'm on hold. Who called?''

''He didn't leave a name. He said he'd get back to you. Is that garden yours? It's nice.''

''It belongs to the building. Nobody goes there much except the super, who takes care of it. Look, Minnesota, how about taking an early lunch? Then you'll be back when I have to leave. There's a coffee shop around the corner.''

''Brunch'' would have been more correct. It was not quite eleven o'clock, but she hadn't eaten much breakfast.

The coffee shop was an unassuming lunch counter.

She ordered a shrimp salad sandwich and iced tea. After this, she would bring her own and save some money.

She took a long way back to the office, walking around the block to enjoy the weather. It was almost summer. A woman in a sleeveless muumuu strolled toward her with five Pekingese dogs. They spread across the sidewalk, crowding Lily to one side. She reached down to pet the nearest, a black ball of fluff.

"Not that one," said the woman. "He bites."

"Thanks for warning me."

"All the others are okay, but that one bites." The woman reeled in her dogs and walked on.

A young man in tank top and shorts bicycled past. Lily admired his muscles, then felt pangs of guilt. She was being unfaithful to Donald.

But Donald had brains. She admired that too. He would be a respected surgeon like his father.

And what would she be? She wanted to count for something in her own right. Donald's mother thought being a respected surgeon's wife was quite enough, but she belonged to a different generation. Besides, none of the Flynns had much social conscience. It was not what they did best.

When she returned to the office, Al was at her desk, shouting at someone over the phone. His free arm waved angrily, jabbing the air. Lily turned to the oriel window, trying not to listen. It was covered with heavy bars to keep out burglars, and faced a tiny areaway a few steps down from the sidewalk. Sitting at her desk in the middle of the room, she would have a stunning view of legs and feet.

He hung up the phone. "Okay, Minnesota, here's the procedure. If anybody calls or comes in who hasn't been here before, get their name, phone number, and what they want. Some kinds of cases I don't take. Others I don't have time for. Just get the info and I'll decide. If it's somebody who's already a client, take a message. Sometimes you might want to record a call. Use this gizmo here."

It was the transcribing machine on the desk. "By law, you're supposed to tell them you're recording. Sometimes I forget to do that."

She wondered if he forgot on purpose.

He showed her where he kept the forms she was to use for taking information. There were several different kinds, some hand drawn, some laboriously created on the IBM typewriter and then photocopied.

"Did you know there's computer software for making forms?" she asked.

"No, I didn't. Here's the number of my car phone. Don't use it unless you have to. I mean a real emergency."

He disappeared for a few minutes, then returned wearing jeans, a yellow knit shirt, and a blue baseball cap. He looked younger than before, and had muscles like the man on the bicycle. At his throat was a glint of gold from a medal or chain.

"Don't let all this overwhelm you," he said. "If

you come across something you can't figure out, leave it. And thanks.''

When he had gone, she explored the office. There was a file cabinet near her desk, filled with case folders. The shelves at the back of the room contained books, curios, and more African violets. There was also an answering machine and a small stereo. When she turned it on, the strains of a Mozart concerto filled the room.

The telephone rang. She reached for it, scrambling to find a letterhead or anything with the name of the firm.

''Barberini Security,'' she answered breathlessly.

''Miz Crocker?'' It was a male voice.

''This is Miss Foster. May I help you?''

The voice wanted Al, and grunted when told he wasn't there.

''Okay, Miz Foster. Tell him Friday night. Seven-thirty. The warehouse. Got that?''

''Will he know which warehouse?''

''Just give him the message, sweetheart.''

She rewrote it neatly on a message pad headed While You Were Out, and left it on Al's desk. The phone rang again.

A loud soprano wailed in her ear. ''You said you'd have those pictures for me Monday. It's already Wednesday and I still didn't get them. What do you expect me to do?''

''If you'll let me know who you are,'' Lily said,

"I'll be sure to tell Mr. Barberini as soon as he gets in."

"I need them *now*. My lawyer's going to court tomorrow. Don't tell me I have to stop by and pick them up myself!"

"I'm afraid I wouldn't know what to give you. I'm new here, and—"

"I don't want to hear your troubles!" the woman screeched. "I'm telling you I need those pictures now! Where is he? Put that detective on the phone."

"I'm sorry, he's out. If you'll give me your name and number—"

"He knows my name and number!" The phone went dead.

Lily searched her desk. She did not find any pictures, only a postcard addressed to Doris Crocker from someone in Calgary.

She tried the file cabinet. Many of the folders had pictures in them. Photos of men, women, children. Blurry shots of trucks being loaded or unloaded. More blurry shots of motel entrances with people coming and going.

A buzzer announced that someone was at the door. Peering through the window, she saw a blob of electric blue.

"Who is it?" she called.

"Is this the detective's office?" asked a female voice. "My name is Mary Whelan. I don't have an appointment, but could I come in?"

Lily opened the door a crack. Mary Whelan must have been in her forties. She had frizzy chestnut hair, a heavy layer of scarlet lipstick, and a sweet smile.

"The detective's not here right now," Lily said. "Is there anything I can do?"

"I'm looking for someone." Mary Whelan sat down in a chair by the desk and crossed her legs. She wore bright blue pumps to match her dress.

Lily picked up a pencil. "What sort of someone?"

"It's a boy I knew in high school. Bobby Decatur. He was my sweetie. We kind of broke up." Tears came into the wide blue eyes. Mary groped in her purse for a tissue.

Bobby Decatur, Lily wrote, drawing the *o* in Bobby as a heart.

"You see, what happened was," the woman continued, "I got married."

"But not to Bobby."

More tears. Whelan shook her head. "I wish I had. He wouldn't have walked out. My husband left me for some little twit half his age."

"Midlife crisis," Lily said.

Mary sobbed. "It makes you feel so rotten. As if you're not good enough. Well, I got over him, but a couple of months ago—" She paused, gulping, as the telephone rang.

It was the same angry voice as before. "You said you'd get right back to me! Are you going to give him my message or not?"

Lily rolled her eyes. "Ma'am, if you'll just tell me who you are, I can pull your file and see if the pictures are in it."

"I want to talk to Al. Give me Al."

"I already told you he's not here. As soon as he calls in, I'll give him your message."

"That's not good enough!" shouted the woman. "You get hold of Al and tell him to call me right away. I mean it!"

Mary watched in fascination. Lily said, "It looks as if I'll have to try calling my boss. This might be an important client. Excuse me."

Al answered on the first ring with an emphatical whisper. "Yes?"

"It's Lily, at the office. There's a woman who keeps calling and screaming that she wants some pictures. She says she needs them right away."

"Didn't I tell you not to call me here unless it's urgent?"

"I didn't know if it was. This woman thinks it is."

"What woman?"

"She won't give her name. She says you'd know it."

"What am I, a mind reader? I have more than one case. And please don't call me again unless we're at war."

Burning with embarrassment, Lily glanced at her visitor. Mary was absorbed in reminiscences. "A couple of months ago we had our twenty-fifth reunion. My high school class. I almost didn't go. I didn't want to go alone, but then I went.''

"And he was there?" Lily asked.

"No, but it brought back memories. I kept asking about him. Nobody knew where he was, or if he's married, or anything.''

"What will you do if he's married?"

"Oh, then I won't bother him. But if he isn't, I'd like to see him again. I can't get him out of my mind.''

"Let me take the information. I'll refer it to my boss.''

Mary had grown up in Rego Park, Queens. She had already checked the phone book. Bobby Decatur wasn't listed.

"I really want to see him," she repeated. "It feels like yesterday that we were together.''

"I'll see what we can do," Lily promised.

Alone again, she turned up the radio. Mozart was over and they were playing "The Blue Danube." She took a few waltz steps, freezing when she heard a key in the lock. He was back early.

Chapter Two

It wasn't Al, but a woman. She was lithe and catlike in a black jersey jumpsuit tied at the waist with a lavender sash. Her mouth was generous in size, her eyes smoky, and her hair silver-blond. Surrounding her was an aroma of citrus, not spicy, but sweet.

The woman stared. "Who are you? Where's Crocker?"

"I'm assuming," Lily said, "that Crocker was his secretary's name? Apparently she died last night. From a stroke."

The black eyes popped. "You're kidding! Oh, poor Crock. He didn't tell me."

"Were you here to see Miss Crocker? Is there anything I can help you with?"

"*Mrs.* Crocker." The newcomer burst into silvery laughter. "I don't think there's much you can do for me, honey. I've been here longer than you have. What are you, a temp?"

"Yes. Lily Foster. Do you mean you work here? They told me it was a one-man office."

"One *man,* yes." Another giggle. "Some man, huh? I've been with him for over a year now. Where did he go?"

"He's out on a job. Where exactly do you work?"

"Mostly outside. I'm an investigator. Rochelle Pulver."

"It's nice to meet you, Rochelle."

"Poor old Crock. I wonder what's going to happen now."

"He put an ad—" Lily began, when the telephone rang.

It was another job seeker. Lily gave her Al's box number.

"You *could* have said that in the ad," grumbled the caller.

"I think it was an afterthought," Lily replied. "This was all very sudden."

She caught Rochelle as she headed toward Al's room. "Do you know anything about a woman who's expecting some pictures? She keeps calling and screaming at me, but she won't give her name."

"I can't imagine who you mean."

"I don't know what to do. She said she's coming

over to get them. I called Al, but he didn't know either. And he got mad at me for bothering him.''

''He's probably on a stakeout. The ringing phone can call attention to him. By the way, I know he's attractive, but don't get your hopes up.''

Lily was too surprised to think of a good answer. ''My hopes are otherwise engaged,'' she answered stiffly. ''In fact, *I* am.''

''Congratulations. I didn't know. I don't see any ring.''

''There isn't any. We decided to put the money toward his education. He's in medical school.'' The engagement had not yet been formalized, but that was nobody's business. It was the intention that counted.

Rochelle, who perhaps hadn't meant to be obnoxious, gave her a friendly grin and continued into Al's office to make a phone call. As she talked, her free hand wandered over the desk, picking up things and examining them, straightening piles of papers as though she owned the place—or owned Al.

Lily busied herself studying the different forms Al had showed her. Each batch was in a specially marked folder: Employee Theft, Missing Person(s), Divorce, Child Custody.

When she looked up again, Rochelle had vanished. From somewhere came the sound of running water. There must have been a bathroom out in the hallway. There would have to be, Lily thought, in any workplace. She could water the African violets when Rochelle finished.

Someone rattled the outside doorknob. Then the buzzer rang.

She remembered what Al had said about crazies. The door was locked, but the rattling knob bothered her. "Who is it?"

"John Morrissey. I have a three-o'clock appointment."

Rochelle came down the hall, thoroughly transformed. She had changed from the black jumpsuit to a sky-blue dress and white cotton blazer.

Lily asked, "What should I do? There's a man at the door who says he has an appointment and Al's going to be gone all afternoon."

"Let him in. Find out what he wants. That's all you can do." Rochelle pulled open the door and left.

Mr. Morrissey was tall and dignified, with thinning gray hair. Something in his expression, or perhaps it was his age, reminded Lily of her father.

"I'm terribly sorry. Mr. Barberini had to leave on an emergency. I think he'll be out most of the day."

"But I have an appointment," Morrissey pleaded.

The telephone let out a warble. When she turned to answer it, two buttons were flashing. Two calls.

She pressed the first button—"Barberini Security. Will you hold, please?"—then the second.

It was a voice that sounded young and male. "Is that job still open, the one that was advertised?"

"Yes, it is. Please send your résumé to our—"

"Wait, can you tell me how much it pays?"

"I don't know. I'm just temporary here."

Mr. Morrissey edged up beside her.

"Sir," she told the caller as a third button began to flash, "I have another call. Let me give you—"

"I'm not a sir!"

"Whatever. Can you hold just a—"

"Wait! Send it where?"

"I'm sorry, just a moment. I'll be right back." She pressed the third button. "Barberini. Will you hold a—"

"No, I will not! I need those pictures now!"

"I understand, but I have to know whose pictures I'm looking for."

"My husband's! Al knows who that is. What are you, some kind of substitute? Let me talk to a real person."

"Ma'am, I discussed this with Mr. Barberini and he can't identify which pictures you mean. We need more information."

The woman crowed triumphantly. "You told me you don't know where he is!"

"I don't." It was true. "You see, everybody has pictures. There are a lot of clients." Four drawers full, although most, according to their labels, were closed cases. "We need to know who you are so we can pull the . . . Oh, just a minute."

The phone had begun to beep. She stood frozen. What did it mean?

"It's that call on hold," Mr. Morrissey said. "It does that to remind you."

"Oh, my heavens, I forgot. I'll get right back to you." She released the hold button.

"That's not very professional, is it?" said Al's voice, "leaving someone dangling on the phone."

"I'm sorry. It got really hectic. There's a Mr. Morrissey here to see you."

"That's what I'm calling about. Reschedule it, will you? And don't leave anybody dangling."

She stared at the darkened phone. She hadn't left the others dangling, she had cut them off. Still holding the receiver, she passed along Al's message.

"He said to reschedule it, Mr. Morrissey, but he didn't say for when. I don't know what his schedule is."

The man's eyes filled with pain. "I wish he could have let me know that."

He had a right to be annoyed. "I guess he forgot," Lily said. "The previous secretary died suddenly and there's been a lot of confusion."

"I'm sorry to hear it. I suppose now I'll have to find someone else. This can't wait."

Al wouldn't want to lose a client, she was sure. "Maybe I can do something to help?"

"I don't know if you can. It's my daughter. She's

missing, and the trail's getting colder every minute. So you see why I can't wait for Mr. Barberini.''

"How old is your daughter?" Lily pictured a two-year-old snatched from her backyard.

"Fourteen. She ran away. It was her decision, I know, but a kid like that doesn't understand what she's up against.''

"Of course not. I'll see—"

The phone rang again. She picked it up and had her ear blasted with fury.

"Madam,'' Lily said when the caller stopped to breathe, "I'm terribly sorry I cut you off. It was an accident. But I still can't help you with those pictures—"

There was a click and then silence. She looked up at Mr. Morrissey.

"That's someone who thinks the world was made for her benefit. Doesn't she realize there are billions of us on this planet?''

His mouth twisted. "I apologize. I was feeling that way myself. The trouble is, a serious problem can make you lose perspective.''

"You haven't lost perspective. It *is* serious.'' She took a questionnaire from the folder marked Missing Person(s). "Tell me about your daughter. Then we'll have the information ready for Mr. Barberini.''

He hesitated, perhaps still wondering if he ought to find a new investigator. Finally he let out a tense breath and began.

"Her name is Debra. Debbie. She's fourteen. Going

through adolescence, I suppose. Everything's a battle, especially with my wife, her stepmother. Last Friday, while I was away on a business trip, she took off.''

His wife had called the police, who so far had not been able to find the girl. They kept saying she'd probably come home by herself.

''But she hasn't,'' he went on. ''I'm afraid a lot of people think running away is a victimless act. It's not. Kids can end up horribly victimized out there on the street. A friend of mine recommended Mr. Barberini. I was supposed to bring a picture of her.'' He took several photos from an envelope and looked at them sadly.

Debbie Morrissey was a wispy, appealing girl with a heart-shaped face and large, dark eyes. Lily took down a description of her, as well as the family's address.

Close friends, the questionnaire asked. *Home. School. Elsewhere.*

He remembered a name. Trisha something. No idea who she was. His wife might know. Anyway, they had told all that to the police.

''I doubt that the police will share it with us,'' Lily said. ''What about boyfriends?''

He looked affronted. ''She's only fourteen.''

''Well . . . okay.'' Let him keep his innocence if he wanted to. ''Tell me, is her mother living?''

''She lives in Saudi Arabia,'' he snapped. So it hadn't been an amicable divorce. ''Her new husband's a petroleum engineer. I hardly think Debbie could get there without any money, but I called anyway. They haven't heard from her.''

His home was in Larchmont, although he worked in the city. Lily asked, "Does your daughter have friends here in New York that she might be staying with?''

He didn't know of any. His eyes glistened. It took his daughter's absence to make him notice her.

She had had an argument with her stepmother just after Morrissey left for Dallas on Thursday night. He had cut short his trip, and now was growing frantic because the police couldn't find his child.

"I'm sure they're trying,'' Lily said. "Sometimes there's so much going on that they get spread kind of thin. We'll hope Mr. Barberini can do better.''

"I heard he's very good.''

After Morrissey left, a stream of calls came in. Two were job applicants. Then a woman who was getting divorced and suspected her husband had assets hidden away. A company called about a job Al had worked on involving the hijacking of trucks. Several people asked for Mrs. Crocker. Lily felt like an interloper.

Between calls, she went in search of water for the African violets. The hallway led past all three rooms to a door that opened into the garden. Directly across the hall from Al's office was the bathroom. It had a pebbled glass window, tightly closed, that looked out toward the garden, and a shower stall hung with a brown plastic curtain. The office must have been a converted apartment, and a nice one at that.

Next to the bathroom was an alcove containing a small refrigerator, a coffee machine, and a microwave oven, but no sink.

As she started back to the reception room, a flash of green appeared outside. It came down the steps from the street and rang the buzzer with furious insistence. Lily scarcely needed to ask who it was, and opened the door reluctantly.

The green was a sheath dress that hung awkwardly on a sticklike figure. Above it was a face obviously tightened by plastic surgery. The hair was deep orange. Sharp black eyes peered out from between two rows of mascara-caked lashes.

"Where's the other girl who works here?"

The voice was the same one that had been shrieking over the telephone all afternoon.

"Do you mean Rochelle?" Lily asked. "Or Mrs. Crocker, who wasn't exactly a girl. I'm afraid she passed away."

The visitor stared, momentarily taken aback. "So now he's got himself a brainless bimbo."

Lily did her best to overlook that. "It seems we're back where we started. Mr. Barberini's still out and I can't help you without further information. Do you see that file cabinet? It's filled with cases just like yours."

My big mouth, she thought as the woman pushed her out of the way and made a dive for the cabinet.

Now she would rummage through the drawers and Al would blame Lily for permitting it.

"Ma'am, excuse me. That's all private material."

"Get your hands off me, bimbo."

Lily stepped back. She had not actually touched the woman.

Mumbling to herself, the visitor ran a bony finger over the drawer labels and pounced. Lily watched the thin arm busily pushing back folders. On it hung a bracelet encrusted with stones that looked like real diamonds.

Nobody walked around New York wearing a lavish display of diamonds. That bracelet alone could be worth thousands.

"Ma'am, I'll be glad to help you if—"

"I don't need your help."

What if she was a blackmailer searching for secrets?

Careful to avoid physical contact, which might bring charges of assault and battery, Lily tried to close the drawer. The woman wedged her arm in among the folders and smirked.

They had reached an impasse that immobilized them both. "This is ridiculous," Lily said. "If you care to wait for Mr. Barberini, I know he'll be glad to help you, but when I mentioned your problem on the phone—"

The triumph darkened into anger. "*I* don't have a problem, young lady, you do. Mr. Barberini's going to hear about this."

Lily noticed that the drawer had a lock. If she could somehow find the key and get that arm out . . .

Sharp pain made her double over with a cry. The woman had jammed a heel into her instep. With Lily off balance, a push sent her to the floor.

"Got 'em!" cackled the visitor, and slammed the drawer shut. "No thanks to you, bimbo." She waved a batch of five-by-sevens.

Lily picked herself up, holding back tears. "Would you like an envelope for those?"

The woman crammed them into her handbag. "I don't want anything from you. And Mr. Barberini will hear how you tried to break my arm." She marched into Al's office, either forgetting or not believing that he wasn't there.

Lily checked her foot for damage. There was a hole in her stocking and the skin was broken, oozing blood. It would need cleaning at once. She hoped there were ice cubes in the refrigerator to ease her pain.

Through the closed bathroom door, she heard the toilet flushing. Before she could look for ice cubes, the phone rang. It was another call about the job.

She had a good view of the lower hallway and the front door, and would be able to see when the woman left. Her foot throbbed. She distracted herself by calling her roommate Charlene at work.

"I've got a temp job," Lily said. "He's a private eye. My agency called this morning after you left."

"A private eye!" Charlene exclaimed. "That's exciting!"

"So far, it's mostly just crazy. And my foot hurts. I'll tell you about that later."

A flurry of motion on the sidewalk caught Lily's eye.

"Do you know there's a woman outside my window with five Pekingese dogs? I saw her earlier. Imagine leashing up all those dogs for a walk."

"And keeping them brushed," said Charlene.

"Anyhow, the reason I'm calling is that my boss is out and I have no idea when he's coming back. I'm alone here, so I can't leave until he does. Will you tell Donald if he calls? I'll try to get him, but I doubt if he's home yet."

She gave Charlene her number and told her it was for emergencies only. "This is my first day here. I can't be getting a lot of personal calls."

Several minutes later, the quintet of dogs walked by again. Still no one appeared in the hallway. After answering two more calls, she went back to see what was happening. The woman might have had a heart attack after all that exertion.

The bathroom was still closed. She listened, then crept closer and put her ear to the door. There was no sound. She knocked softly.

"Ma'am? Are you there? Are you all right?"

She knocked again and tried the knob. It turned.

The door opened a few inches and then stopped.

Something blocked the way. Something that gave reluctantly when she pushed against it. A foot.

The woman lay on her side, her knees bent and right arm flung out. The diamond bracelet was gone. Around her neck was a yellow scarf, tightly pulled.

Chapter Three

Police and paramedics swarmed through the office.

"It's a good thing you loosened that scarf," one of them told Lily. "She could be gone by now if you hadn't."

"I thought she *was* gone." Lily still felt dazed. "It took me awhile to find her pulse. But how did anybody get in here? I would have seen them come through the front door."

The police checked the garden, the hallway, and all three rooms of the office. They grilled the building superintendent, José Rodriguez, who claimed he hadn't been on the premises when it happened. He had two other buildings to take care of, he said.

They interrogated Lily for everything she knew. The

29

victim's name, she discovered, was Hortense Lanken. Still unconscious, the woman had been taken to Bellevue Hospital. The paramedics thought she would live.

Lily gave the police Al's car phone number. If this didn't qualify as war, the only condition on which he would allow himself to be disturbed, she could not imagine what did. He would be irate at having his stakeout interrupted. He would be furious that she had let this happen, and on her first day of work—which was probably also her last.

It was well past five o'clock, and she was still at her desk taking phone calls, when he came in. She knew Donald would be waiting for her, but did not want to call Charlene or Pat, her other roommate, and have to explain. It was better to save that for later when she could do it in person.

She waited, not knowing whether she might still be needed. When Al had finished talking with the police, he came out to the reception room and sat down in the chair by her desk. "Okay, let's hear what happened."

"The police didn't tell you?"

"The police don't give out information. They only ask questions. Didn't you notice anything? Hear anything?"

She hadn't thought about that. "All I heard was the toilet flushing. I didn't think it was so unusual."

"It's not," he said. "Lanken has a bladder problem. She always pays a visit to the girls' room."

Lily gave him a full account of Mrs. Lanken's visit.

Her description of the woman's behavior did not surprise him.

"She's kind of a nut," he explained. "Rich, though. It was her money that got him started."

"Got who started?"

"Her husband. Barry Lanken, the TV producer."

Lily had never heard of him. The Lankens were divorcing, Al said, and Mrs. Lanken had hired him to "get the goods" on her husband. One of his part-timers had managed to take some incriminating photos. They were what Mrs. Lanken had been after.

"What do you mean by 'incriminating'?" Lily asked. "With other women?"

"That's exactly what I mean. The guy's in TV, so there's wall-to-wall actresses trying to get his attention. He's a real personality boy, a lot better-looking than his wife. It's too much for a guy to resist."

"That's no excuse." But Lily could scarcely blame him for being able to resist his wife. "She had on a bracelet that I thought was diamond. I told that to the police. It was missing when I found her. Why would anybody go out in public with real diamonds?"

"She does that kind of thing," he said. "I've warned her. Probably other people have too."

"Somebody must have noticed it on her, but I still don't understand how they got in. I would have seen them. Is the back door kept locked?"

"Usually, unless somebody's out there, and it's limited access anyway. Your intruder would have to get into one of the other buildings on this block and climb over a high, spiky fence. There's a passageway from the street where José takes out the garbage, but it's got a heavy iron gate that's always locked. Only José has a key.''

"Maybe somebody slipped in when he had it open?''

"He wouldn't be taking out garbage in the afternoon," Al said. "He does it at night.''

"The police questioned him.''

"They would. He'd be pretty obvious, since he has access. But I know José. He wouldn't do a thing like that even for a diamond bracelet.''

She had seen José only briefly. He was a heavyset man, perhaps in his fifties, with a round, sad face. Secretly she thought a lot of people might be tempted by such easy prey, but José would also know that he'd be an obvious suspect.

"Why don't you go on home?'' Al suggested. "Let's hope tomorrow's a better day. Or at least quieter.''

"Do you want me to come back tomorrow?'' Her first day had been such a disaster.

"Why not? I need somebody here, and you've already had some experience. Besides . . . '' His eyes twinkled, although the rest of his face didn't change. "You proved you can handle a crisis.''

"Thank you. I'll see you tomorrow then.''

In late spring, it was still light outside. She wouldn't have liked the dark on that particular day as she walked to Fourteenth Street and took the subway to Sixty-eighth.

Her apartment building, on East Seventy-first Street, was a large one with a doorman. Donald had insisted that she have a doorman for safety. The only way Lily could afford such a place was by sharing it, and so she had moved in with Charlene Peters, a friend from high school, and her roommate, Pat Cotton.

She smelled coffee as soon as she unlocked the apartment door. Pat and Charlene were entertaining Donald, who had been waiting for her to come home.

Three faces turned toward her when she entered the living room. Charlene, blond and dimpled, sat holding her coffee mug like a society matron at tea. Elfin Pat was sprawled on the sofa next to her tennis racket.

Donald unfolded himself gracefully from his chair. "What happened to you? I thought you got mugged or something. You scared me to death."

Donald had the looks and assurance of a male model, and the smile of Tom Cruise. Lily murmured an apology, received a kiss on her forehead, and started toward her bedroom to repair the day's damage.

Charlene screeched, "What happened to your foot?"

"Somebody stepped on it in the subway," Lily said. She had planned to tell them about Mrs. Lanken, but suddenly it seemed too lurid. Donald would never let her go back to work in a place of mayhem and attempted murder.

"Did you eat?" asked Pat.

"I'm fine." Eating was the last thing Lily wanted to do, with memories of a half dead Mrs. Lanken still so vivid. Even the box of chocolate chip cookies on the coffee table sickened her.

Charlene pushed the box toward her. "How do you like working for a private eye?"

"It's mostly answering the telephone and filling out questionnaires. But you get to meet a variety of people." Lily averted her eyes from the cookies, but the smell was still there.

"What sort of people?"

"There was a man whose daughter ran away, a woman looking for some old boyfriend, and another woman divorcing her husband because he chased skirts. Or maybe the skirts chased him. I wasn't too clear on that. No, thanks. No coffee. I've had enough excitement today."

She hadn't meant to say it. Charlene pounced. "What do you mean?"

"Nothing, really. One of our clients got sick in the bathroom and I had to help her." Lily was glad when Donald set down his cup.

"Walk over to the river?" he suggested, forgetting her injured foot.

"Just give me a minute to change my shoes." An evening walk was the only way they could be alone together. Quickly she medicated her foot, put on a pair of comfortable flats, and took an aspirin to ease the discomfort.

They strolled along Seventy-first Street to the East River, whose surface reflected the lights of Queens Borough, stretching them out like tall candle flames. The air was soft, the twilight hazy and mauve.

"One of our clients lives over there," Lily said. "She came in today looking for her high school boyfriend. She called him her sweetie."

"I thought you weren't going to take any more temp jobs."

"I wasn't. But they called me this morning and I needed the money. He's looking for somebody permanent. Do you think I should apply?"

Donald's mouth curled with distaste. "Answering phone calls for a detective? You can do better than that."

"What makes you think so? I haven't so far. Maybe I'd better break down and learn word processing. I was afraid I'd get stuck doing it forever, but it's better than nothing."

"I think you should just be patient," he said. "Something else will come along like that magazine job."

"Donald, I need money *now*. I can't even pay my share of the rent, much less save anything for law school."

"Still on that law school kick?" He chuckled fondly as he pulled her down onto a bench. "You'll have enough to do as soon as we're married and have kids."

"Let's not have them right away. I'd like a little time just for us. In fact . . . "

He waited for her to continue. She wished she hadn't begun.

"I'd like to get my life in order. I want to matter as a human being. I want to count for something."

His arm dropped from around her shoulder. "Are you saying you don't? You're going to be my wife. What's wrong with that?"

She hadn't expected him to understand. "It's hard to explain."

"Go on. I'm interested."

"You're going to be a doctor, helping people." Although she couldn't be sure that was his primary motive. "I want to do something worthwhile too. If I go into law, I can work with people who are helpless and in trouble."

He brightened. "As my wife, you'll be helping me so *I* can help people. But if law school makes you happy, then go for it. It might be kind of amusing to have a wife studying law."

"I wasn't thinking of it as amusement. Anyway, even if this job isn't prestigious, it's interesting. Better than a lot of things I've done."

His arm slipped back around her. "That's good. I want you to be happy. But I know something better will come along. Hup!"

That meant they were to get up off the bench and

start home. The mauve dusk had vanished and it was nighttime now. A mild, sparkling city night.

Donald kissed her good-bye at the entrance to her building. His job at the hospital started early in the morning.

"I'm sorry we didn't have more time," Lily said. "It's only for a few days, and I'm sure they won't all be like this."

"They'd better not be." He kissed her again. "Or I'll come storming in there and take you away."

Oscar, the doorman, nodded a greeting as he let her in. He seemed uneasy. His eyes dug into hers with a strange intensity, as though they carried a hidden message. Maybe she imagined it.

When she was halfway to the elevator, two men emerged from the alcove where the mailboxes were. Startled, she could only stare at them. One was a detective who had questioned her that afternoon. Muldoon, she thought his name was.

They showed her their badges. Muldoon said, "Miss Foster, we'd like you to come downtown with us."

She looked back at Oscar. He turned away.

"What for?" she asked. "I already told you everything."

"We'd like you to answer a few more questions about the assault on Mrs. Lanken," Muldoon replied.

"But I don't know anything else. Really."

"I think you do, Miss Foster. You've been identified as the person who assaulted her."

Chapter Four

Numbly, she watched the lights of Third Avenue pass by. Muldoon hadn't said where they were taking her. Just "downtown." She could not believe this was happening.

"Who identified me?" she asked.

They wouldn't tell her.

She could only hope Oscar would keep his mouth shut. Doormen were supposed to be discreet. She did not want any of the other tenants to know, least of all her roommates. She did not want her parents to know. Or Donald. Or Donald's parents.

She closed her eyes. The city lights, which had enchanted her only minutes earlier, had lost their charm.

"I want a lawyer," she said. "But I don't know any. What should I do?"

Muldoon turned partway from the front seat, showing his flattened nose in profile. "You're not under arrest, Miss Foster. We just want to ask some questions."

She knew the Miranda rights, which they would read to her if she were arrested. But what were the rights of a person who was only being questioned?

By the time they reached the police station, she had made up her mind. "I would like to notify someone of where I am. I don't want to get lost in the system."

"You won't get lost in the system," Muldoon assured her. "We're only asking questions. Then you can go."

Unless they arrest me. "I would like to notify my boss, but I don't have his home phone number. I'm sure it must be in the notes you took."

"I'm sorry. We can't give out that information."

"Then I want to call his office." She could leave a message on the answering machine. That way, if she wasn't there in the morning, he would know why.

They allowed her to make the call. Then they took her to a small room with bare walls and one high window. The only furnishing was a large table with several chairs around it.

They were joined by another officer and someone with a tape recorder. Muldoon asked Lily to describe the afternoon from the moment of Mrs. Lanken's arrival. She had already given him that information back at the office. She went over it again, starting with the first phone call.

"Even Mr. Barberini didn't know who I was talking about, but I couldn't get that through to this woman. She kept yelling and screaming and making demands, and finally said she was coming to find them herself."

Lily had already supplied them with the details of that encounter. They wanted to hear it again, this time with the tape recorder running.

"After she got hold of the pictures, she went into Mr. Barberini's office. I figured she wouldn't find him there, and she'd leave. He has a door that opens directly into the hallway. She must have gone out that way to the bathroom."

She described how she had squeezed into the room and found Mrs. Lanken on the floor. She had felt for a pulse, then loosened the cloth around her neck. "I pumped her chest a couple of times and she started breathing. I guess she must have been breathing all along, but it wasn't noticeable. Then I called 911."

"Did anybody else know Mrs. Lanken was there?"

"I told Rochelle Pulver she was coming, because I didn't know what to do about it. She didn't either. Anyway, she left before Mrs. Lanken got there. Quite awhile before."

"Did anyone else come in while Mrs. Lanken was there?"

"Nobody. I would have seen them. We keep the

front door locked, so I'd have had to let them in. And only that building has access to the garden.''

''The garden?''

''The backyard.''

They left her alone for a while. What if they didn't believe her? What if she really did get arrested and booked?

Who had identified her as the assailant? If anyone saw her go into the bathroom, it must have been the attacker himself.

Finally they said she could leave. It was almost midnight. She was not even sure where she was, and she would never take the subway at that hour. She counted the bills in her wallet to see if there was enough for a taxi.

''I'll drive you home, Minnesota.''

Al stood lounging against a wall just inside the entrance to the station.

''What are you doing here?'' she asked.

''I got your message. And I feel kind of responsible for you being in this mess.''

He had on the same baseball cap and jeans, but had changed his shirt. It was a white one this time, with a penguin on the pocket.

''Do you usually work this late?'' she asked.

''No, I was home, but I call in now and then to pick up my messages. What happened?'' He took her elbow and led her outside. She still didn't know where they were.

"Somebody identified me as the person who attacked Mrs. Lanken," she said. "Maybe they really thought I did it, but the police wouldn't tell me who it was."

"How about some coffee?" he suggested. "Something to help you unwind."

"Coffee doesn't help me unwind, but I haven't eaten since lunch. I didn't feel like it till now. All because of Mrs. Lanken."

"There's an all-night hamburger place nearby. Is that okay?"

Anything was okay. The hamburger place was pleasantly bright, done in cream and pink Formica, with plastic hanging plants. She ordered a cheeseburger, fries and cole slaw, and a glass of 7-Up.

"How come the police let me go if somebody thinks they saw me do it?" she asked.

"Nobody saw you do it."

"But they said—"

"Your unreliable witness was Mrs. Lanken herself. She didn't see a thing and has no memory of the actual event, but she fingered you because you were the only one there."

"How does she know I was the only one there? To me, it's obvious somebody else was too. People shouldn't make accusations on such flimsy reasoning."

"Mrs. Lanken does a lot of things she shouldn't do, including running around in diamond bracelets."

"I saved her life! The paramedics said so. I could

have just called an ambulance and never bothered touching her. Especially after the way she treated me.''

''I believe you, Lily.''

''Thanks. And thanks for calling me Lily. I'm sure Minnesota would be a nice name if it were appropriate, but it isn't.''

''That was my first impression of you,'' he said. ''It kind of stuck. Would you rather be called New Jersey?''

''It makes me think of Jersey cows. I'd rather be called Lily.''

Her cheeseburger arrived. It was juicy and comforting, but she still could not get over Mrs. Lanken.

''How could she do that? If my fiancé's parents ever hear that I was taken in for questioning . . . You don't know my fiancé's parents. Even *he* . . . I mean, it's so awful, being accused of a crime. That's why I want to study law. To help people like me. And what if my parents find out?''

''They won't.''

''What makes you so sure? You said Mr. Lanken's a big shot in TV. I happen to know reporters lurk around waiting for this kind of dirt.''

''It's true,'' said Al. ''Reporters often do hang around police stations looking for breaking news, but the police aren't going to talk while it's under investigation. Besides, I told them to keep you out of it.''

''They'll listen to you?''

"I think so. I used to be one of them. Tell me about this boyfriend of yours."

"Donald. He's in med school. Next year he'll start interning. That's probably when we'll get married. He's gorgeous. Comes from a good family, and he's going to be a surgeon. He's everything my parents dreamed of."

"Your parents are going to marry him?"

"Oh, you know. For me. They wanted me to have the best. I guess every parent does. But that's sort of quaint, don't you think? A good marriage is okay, but it's not really an achievement. I'd rather accomplish something on my own."

"So you're planning on law school. Did you always want to be a lawyer?"

"No, that was recent." She sprinkled salt on her French fries. "I wanted to be all sorts of things when I was a kid. An astronaut. A college professor. A nurse. For a while, I even thought of being a clergywoman. I just wanted to matter."

He stirred half a packet of sugar into his coffee. "What do your folks do?"

"My mom's a bank officer. My dad works for a company that makes electric signs. He commutes to the city. My sister's a dental assistant. She's married. My brother's in high school. What about you? How did you get into detective work?"

"I was a cop."

"Aren't you kind of young to be retired?"

"I didn't retire. I resigned. There were reasons." It was all he would say.

"What about your folks?" she asked. "What sort of family do you have?"

"Italian."

"No, really? I never would have guessed."

"I guessed you were Swedish, and it turns out you're not. So what does that prove?"

"If you weren't Italian, I'd have eaten my . . . cheese-burger. But I mean, where did you grow up? What do your parents do? I told you everything about me. Now it's your turn."

"I grew up on Bleecker Street," he said. "Little Italy. My dad was a bartender. He died a few years ago. Lung cancer. Bars are filled with smoke. My mom never held a job. She spends her time cooking. Nice, rich Italian food. I have five brothers and sisters. She's always stuffing them and their families."

"What about you and your family?"

"Don't have one. Not yet." Again he closed up.

"Thank you for dinner. It really helps."

"You're entirely welcome." They went out to his car, a five-year-old gray Honda, and he drove her home.

"Nice building," he said as he stopped in front of it.

So that he wouldn't misunderstand her finances, she explained about the roommates and how Donald wanted her to be safe.

"Am I out of the woods yet with the police?" she asked.

"I think they'll be keeping an eye on you. They can't ignore the fact that she fingered you, even without any basis. So you may still be a suspect."

"I think it's ridiculous."

"Yes, it is. They've put out an alert on the bracelet. Sooner or later somebody'll try to fence it. That should give them a lead. So don't lose sleep over it, okay?" He gave her arm a squeeze as she got out of the car.

By then, Oscar had gone off duty. The night man opened the door for her, beaming a friendly smile, but that did not erase the memory of her earlier experience.

She had always been on the side of law and order and still believed in it. But she could understand the frustration of those wrongly accused.

Chapter Five

Lily woke the next morning to the smell of burning sugar. Another Pop-Tart had gotten stuck in the toaster.

Charlene had everything under control and was sitting at the table eating breakfast. "What did you do last night? You must have come in after we went to bed. I thought Donald was an early bird."

Lily poured a cup of coffee while she waited for Pat to finish in the shower. She was not yet awake enough to deal with this.

Any excuse that involved Donald ran the risk of being blown. Her roommates saw too much of him, and talked too much.

"It was such a nice night," she finally replied, "I felt like taking a walk."

"By *yourself?* At *night?*"

"There were thousands of people around. Nothing to worry about."

"Did you have a fight with Donald? I can't see walking around by yourself unless there was something on your mind."

"It had nothing to do with Donald. I was trying to figure out how I can afford law school with no money. Why can't she blow-dry her hair in the bedroom?"

Fortunately Pat didn't have much hair, only a short, black cap, and the drying was over quickly. Lily wondered if she could ever bring herself to tell them the truth. It wasn't as if she had actually been arrested. It was not even her fault, but she couldn't help feeling tainted by it.

She reached the office at eight forty-five, after a crowded subway ride. Al was there alone and buzzed her in. He mumbled something about giving her a key.

She stored her tuna sandwich in the refrigerator, then went to the bathroom to wash her hands. It was similar to getting back on a horse after falling off. She couldn't be spooked by that room forever, but it was hard not to think of Mrs. Lanken lying crumpled on the floor.

The door could be locked by a button in the knob. Might Mrs. Lanken have forgotten to press it? How could anyone forget to lock a bathroom door in a semi-public place?

There was the window, but it was too narrow for

most people to squeeze through. If anyone did, it would be a struggle, and Mrs. Lanken would surely notice. Lily remembered that the window had been closed tight, perhaps even painted shut, and the dust on its sill undisturbed.

Now the dust was nearly gone. Probably the police had done that. They had been all over looking for clues, and if they hadn't found anything, it meant there was nothing to find. They were trained to know what to look for.

She returned to her desk and answered the ringing phone. It was Mr. Morrissey, asking for Al.

She pressed the hold button and called through the vacant middle room, "It's that man with the runaway daughter."

The questionnaire she had filled out was still on her desk. She took it in to Al while he talked.

"Yes . . . yes," she heard him say. "I do apologize. . . . Well, no, it looks as if my assistant got the basics here. I want to talk to your wife, though. Yes, we have the number. I'll be in touch."

When the call was finished, Lily showed him the information on Mary Whelan.

"She wants to find her high school sweetheart. They haven't seen each other in twenty-five years. She says if he's married she'll leave him alone, but she can't get him out of her mind."

Al skimmed over the paper. "She'll leave him alone if he's married, but she can't get him out of her mind?"

"That's what she said. I know she's romanticizing, but if it does turn out he's married, it might bring her back to reality."

"Or it might not. I'll tell you, Lily, I don't usually take this kind of case. In the first place, it's frivolous."

"Frivolous? To look for someone you love?"

"Compared with other things. The Morrissey kid, for instance, could be in danger. That's what I don't consider frivolous."

"I understand. I know you can't take everything that comes along."

"There's another problem too with this kind of case." He handed back the Whelan questionnaire. "It can cause trouble. Their relationship's been over for a long time. Whatever she feels about it, he's undoubtedly made a life for himself, probably has a wife and kids, and here's this lovesick woman barging into his life—"

"She said she'd leave him alone."

"Sure she did. But people don't always do what they say. I'm not getting into this."

Lily persisted. "What if he's been pining for her all these years?"

"Yeah, right," said Al.

"It could happen."

"Drop it, okay?"

You might make two people very happy. "Do I have to tell her you won't take the case?"

"If you don't, she'll be waiting around for something that's not going to happen."

Mary Whelan would be at work now. She was a secretary for a trucking company in Long Island City. She must have taken time off for yesterday's visit, coming all the way into Manhattan. It was that important to her. Why couldn't she meet some nice trucker and settle down?

Because she was too hung up on Bobby Decatur and couldn't look at anyone else. Al was right. It would be better just to break it to her and let her get on with her life.

Mary was stunned. "He won't take my case? Why?"

"He has a very heavy workload right now," Lily said. "He really can't take on any more."

"I could wait until he's not so busy. I've waited all this time. All these years."

"Mrs. Whelan, I really—"

"*Miss* Whelan. I use my maiden name now."

"I see. Anyway, I think it would be better . . . I mean, people change. You might not even like your friend any more."

"But I have to know. You can understand that. You seem like a sensitive person. I have to know what Bobby's doing now, and how he is. I have to see him."

Maybe she really did, in order to get over him.

"I'll be glad to wait awhile," Mary said again, "until Mr. Barberini has more time."

"I can't tell you when that will be. He has a long

waiting list. . . . '' This was getting worse and worse. Lily turned to check on Al. He sat with the phone to his ear, diddling on the computer.

She lowered her voice. ''I'll tell you what. Let me see what I can do, and I'll get back to you.''

''Would you? Do you think he could squeeze it in? I tried the phone book already, but I couldn't find Bobby and I don't know what to do now.''

Lily made up her mind as she spoke. ''*If* we're able to find him, here's what we're going to do. We'll approach him first and see what he has to say. If he wants to get in touch with you, we'll give him your address. Otherwise, we'll let it go at that.''

''Aren't you going to tell me where he is?'' Mary begged.

''It wouldn't be ethical,'' said Lily. ''But I promise you a full report, everything except his whereabouts.''

''Could you get me a picture of him?''

''We'll see what he says about that. Don't you have a yearbook?''

''I want to know what he looks like now.''

The woman was nuts, but Lily could sympathize. She knew what love felt like. ''That's up to him. But I'll ask.''

''Oh, thank you, dear. Thank you so much! I'll be waiting to hear from you.''

Lily buried her face in her hands. Then she realized Al could see her. She did not want him wondering what the trouble was.

She caught him between phone calls. "I'm curious. How do you go about finding a person if you don't know where to look?"

"What are you talking about?" he asked. "If you have to find somebody, it's almost always because you don't know where they are."

"Well, the Morrissey girl, for instance. How do you start?"

"You start with the last anyone saw of her. Time, place, her frame of mind. What she talked about. What she wore and what she might have taken with her. How much money she had. You check out her friends, and the friends of friends. Any possible contacts. In the case of a runaway, a lot of them are going to stonewall to protect her. Kids have this Us against Them thing, with Them being all adults, so you have to work at it. You have to point out that what they're doing could hurt the girl and even get themselves in trouble."

It was all very interesting, but it didn't help her much. "What about an adult?"

"An adult runaway? Same thing, pretty much."

"I mean an adult that somebody's lost touch with. How do you find them?"

His eyes narrowed. "Did you talk to that woman and tell her I'm not taking the case?"

"Yes, but I'm still curious. Say you did take a case like that, how would you go about it?"

"Lily, I don't have time for this now. If you're interested, read a book on it. Take a course."

"What kind of course?"

"The College of Criminal Justice has courses. And there are some books back there." He waved toward a shelf in the corner of his office. She picked one that was titled *How to Find Out Anything about Anybody* and hurried back to answer the phone.

It was Morrissey again. Al spoke briefly with him, and then spent the next hour making multiple calls. Meanwhile, the phone kept ringing. There were inquiries about the job: There was a man who said he was one of Al's part-time investigators. Then Rochelle called.

"I'm sorry, he's on another line," said Lily. "I really wish you'd stayed here yesterday, Rochelle."

"Why, what happened?" The voice was sultry and amused.

"You didn't hear?" Perhaps she was not so chummy with Al after all. Lily told her about Mrs. Lanken's misadventure, leaving out her own role as suspect.

"My goodness, the poor old duck," Rochelle said. "Did Al send her flowers at the hospital?"

"He didn't say anything about it. I'll ask him."

Rochelle hung up without leaving a message. Lily wrote one anyway. *Rochelle called. Flowers for Lanken?* She went in and placed it on Al's desk. He nodded, still on the phone.

When she returned to the front room, the phone was ringing again, flashing its light. As she picked it up, a woman sobbed, ''Please! You've got to help me find my children!''

Chapter Six

Al stood over her desk. "Call Morrissey and ask him to meet me at Canal and Clinton. I'm leaving now."

"Will he know where it is?" Lily asked.

"Canal Street, right? Clinton is a few blocks north of the Manhattan Bridge. It's a continuation of Avenue B. He should get there as soon as possible."

Seeing her bewilderment, he said, "Even if I find the girl, I'm prohibited by law from kidnapping her. With her father there, we'll be taking her into his custody, not mine."

"You found her already?"

"Maybe." He started toward the door, pulling the

baseball cap over his head. It looked incongruous with his suit.

"Oh, Al. Some woman called and wants you to find her children. She thinks her ex-husband kidnapped them."

He groaned.

"I took her number," Lily said. "What should I tell her?"

"Tell her to come in and bring some pictures of the kids and her ex, if she has one. Take the information, but get hold of Morrissey first. I'm out of here."

Mr. Morrissey, when she reached him, all but cried with relief. He was willing to cancel an important appointment to get his daughter back.

"What does Barberini look like?" he asked.

She described Al as best she could, down to the thin scar at the side of his mouth. "He's wearing a blue baseball cap and a tan suit today, but he might have the jacket off. A teal-blue tie. He's quite good-looking." She smiled to herself, glad that Al was not there to hear her.

"Does he know what I look like?" Morrissey asked.

"Yes. You were in one of the pictures you gave us."

"I appreciate this very much."

He really loved his daughter. If only he would learn to show more interest in her.

Another job hunter called. Then it was Rochelle again, asking impatiently, "Is he still on the phone?"

"Actually, he's gone out."

"Oh. Did you ask him about the flowers?"

"I didn't have a chance. He was rushing."

"Okay, I'll take care of it. Whatever happened to those pictures she was after? Did you get them back?"

"She put them in her purse," Lily said. "I really didn't think about the pictures when I found her."

"Oh, well. I just hope she got the right ones. Take care, hon."

Lily put through a call to Detective Muldoon, although he was the last person, aside from Mrs. Lanken, that she wanted to talk to.

Muldoon was not in his office. She spoke with someone named Washington and left a message asking if the pictures had been found in Lanken's purse.

She called Susan Harding, the woman whose children were missing. Susan wanted to come over at once. Lily readied one of the Missing Person(s) forms, then discovered there was another for Custodial Interference.

While waiting for Susan, she looked through the book *How to Find Out Anything about Anybody*.

Of course. Start with the high school. She didn't think high schools kept track of their alumni the way colleges did, but it wouldn't hurt to try. Perhaps Mary Whelan already had.

What were Bobby Decatur's interests that might lead to a career? Who were his best friends? His family's friends, and their former neighbors in Rego Park? She needed a lot more information. As she was about to call and ask, the doorbell rang. Susan Harding lived and worked only a few blocks away.

She was young, with a pale face and violet eyes. She wore a cotton print dress and no makeup. Dark wavy hair fell shapelessly to her shoulders.

"Mr. Barberini's out right now," Lily said, "finding a runaway teenager. But I can take down all your information and get this thing going."

Susan's worry lines eased. "Is he really good at finding people?"

"He does it for a living, so I guess he must be."

Susan held out a photograph but couldn't let go of it. "These are my children. As you can see, they're just babies." Her voice broke. "Kevin's three and Stacey's only eighteen months."

Lily passed her a box of tissues she had found in a drawer and took one for herself. "When did they disappear and how can you be sure he has them?"

"It was him, all right. He had his visitation day two weeks ago Saturday. When he didn't bring them back, I knew. He was living with a friend of his. The friend came home that day and found him gone. All his stuff was gone too."

"Does the friend have any ideas?"

"Nothing. He said George never told him what he planned to do."

Lily took the friend's name and address. He worked

for an insurance company, Susan said, and was also divorced, but childless.

"What about your husband?" asked Lily. "What does he do for a living?" She knew that people could often be traced through their professions. Most needed an income, and it wasn't easy to pick up new job skills in a hurry.

Susan took a fresh tissue. "He teaches high school. He was a math teacher. I don't know what he's doing now."

"Public high school? Here in the city? Then he must belong to the union."

"No, it was a private school. Bristol Academy on Twenty-third Street. I know they aren't unionized."

Lily crossed off the word *union* that she had just written. "Are his parents living? Brothers and sisters?"

"His mother works at a hotel on Saint Thomas. She says she hasn't heard from him. He doesn't have any brothers or sisters."

"What have the police been doing, do you know?"

"They're trying. The FBI too. They checked the Virgin Islands, the airlines. Everywhere, I guess. A friend of mine said I should try a private investigator."

"Does your husband have a car?"

Susan wiped her eyes. "Not that I know of. We never had one in the city. But anyway, you can't get to the islands by car."

"I realize that. He probably wouldn't go there anyway. It would be too obvious. Of course he could have used a different name. He could disguise the children. I suppose the police already checked for credit card use.'' Lily wondered what Al could do that the police hadn't already tried.

"He might have rented a car," Susan said.

"Do you know what credit cards he has?"

"I know what we both had before we divorced. He could have gotten a new one."

Al would know how to find that out. Lily asked, "Isn't there a computer network for missing children?"

"I think so. The National Crime Computer, but what good is it if it doesn't find my kids? They've been gone two weeks already. That's a lot of time. They could be in Morocco by now."

Lily patted her arm. "Not without a passport."

"I don't mean he *went* to Morocco. That was just a for instance." Susan choked on a gulping sob. "But even if he never left the United States, there's all that space to cover. There are a lot of places he could be."

"What do you know about your husband's friends? Especially his special friends, or people he knew before you were married. Excuse me for asking, but what was the reason for your breakup? Was he seeing someone? I'm sorry to be nosy, but I have to do it."

Susan dabbed at another tear. "It was because . . . well, he started drinking. It made him nasty. He never hit me, but his words hurt so much. I tried to live with it, I kept hoping he'd stop, but it got worse. He began yelling at the kids. He was mean and sarcastic and he slapped Kevin for no reason. I'm so afraid for them.''

"I can see what you mean." *Abusive,* Lily wrote. Almost certainly he had taken the children to spite his wife, not because he really wanted them.

"He must have bought them new clothes," said Susan. "They didn't have anything else with them. It was just a day visit. He might have changed their hair color too. I've heard of that happening."

"Yes," Lily agreed. "He could even do a gender switch. Pass them off as two girls or two boys. First we'll have to narrow it down to where he might have gone. Do you know his Social Security number?"

"Yes, I have it. I didn't know it before. The police got it from his employer."

"Ah, yes. The employer." But the police would have tried that lead too. And they had a two-week headstart. It was hopeless to think Al could do any better.

While she ate her tuna sandwich, Lily reviewed the material she had gotten, including the photo of an arrogant-looking man in sunglasses. Where would a person who looked like that take his children? Dark glasses could be worn anywhere, but for some reason she thought of the Sun Belt. He did, according to Susan, have a cousin in Arizona. Susan was going to call later with specific names, addresses, and phone numbers.

The front door opened. It was Rochelle Pulver, this time in white tights and a hot pink tunic.

"Al's not back yet?"

"Not yet," said Lily. "I did tell him you called." She could not take her eyes off the gold filigree belt that held in the tunic. "How do you keep your waist so thin? It's incredible."

"Exercise. I'm a dancer. What have you got here?" Rochelle picked up the form Lily had filled out for Susan Harding.

"Kid snatch, huh? He doesn't like those, you know."

Lily remembered how Al had groaned when she told him about the case. "He said to get the information. Why doesn't he like them?"

"Too much travel. They always go someplace far away and it means dropping everything else. If he's taking it, I hope you got a retainer."

"He never said anything about that."

"Honey, he always needs a retainer. A thousand up front, usually. It's not only expenses, it's a guarantee. You'd be surprised how stingy some people are. As soon as their case is solved, they don't want to pay him." Rochelle dropped the questionnaire back on Lily's desk and tapped it with a long, silver fingernail. "I'll bet you never even discussed money with her."

"Well, no, I didn't," Lily admitted. "Even if it occurred to me, I wouldn't have known what to say. I don't know what he charges."

"Yeah, I guess. It's hard to learn when nobody's

here to teach you. I just hope she doesn't get too difficult.''

Lily hoped so too. "I didn't know you were a dancer. Where do you dance?''

''Broadway, when I can get it.''

''Really? Broadway? Do you mean in musicals?''

''That's where the dancing is. In musicals, like you might expect. There's a lot of competition, but I've been in a couple of shows.''

''I should think that would take all your time and energy. How do you manage to do investigating too?''

''Investigating pays the rent. I don't especially care to be homeless. Well, I'm off to an audition. Tell Al I stopped by to see if he has anything.''

''Good luck with your audition!'' Lily called after her.

Al came back late in the afternoon, wilted and discouraged. His tie was loosened and his jacket slung over one shoulder.

''We spotted the girl but couldn't get her,'' he reported. ''Have to try again tomorrow. She's around there someplace, but we don't have an exact address.''

''Do you think she saw you?'' Lily asked as she handed him his phone messages.

''It's hard to say. She might have been alerted. As long as she doesn't leave the area, we'll be okay.''

He took the messages into his office. Soon a phone

button lit up. It was ten after five. Donald would be fidgeting, but she couldn't help that.

When Al finished his calls, she gave him the sheet she had made out for Susan Harding. "Rochelle stopped by to see if you have any work for her. She said you don't like to take this kind of case."

Without replying, he read over what she had written, including the names of Harding's friends, which Susan had given her later by phone.

"Okay." He leaned back, closing his eyes.

"Can I make you some coffee?" Lily asked.

"No, I'll be fine. It's just one of those days."

"Anything I can do to help with these kids? Their mother's really upset."

"Tomorrow. You can do plenty then. These people"—he thumped the questionnaire—"all have to be checked. You're going to call them with . . . Let's see, what kind of inducement can we offer? Maybe he won a sweepstakes, or something."

"Wouldn't he know if he entered one?"

"Somebody could have entered for him. Don't tell them about it directly, make it oblique, just so his friends get the idea. Whatever else they might be cautious about, they'll want to help him get his hands on money. Everybody needs money."

"Any particular sweepstakes?" she asked.

"Make up one. You're going to be a sweepstakes representative. You'll figure out a whole story about that, an identity for yourself, but it's got to be plausible.

No holes, nothing unrealistic. What you're really doing is listening for reactions. That's probably all you'll get.''

"How do I do that?''

He glared at her. "Use your intuition. Women are supposed to be good at that. Now, with each of these people, you're going to act like you know he's there, or that he gave that particular name as a contact. This is the sort of thing I like to use Rochelle for. She's an actress. You can't have any wavering or uncertainty.''

"I can do that.''

"You're sure? With each one, remember, that's the place he said he was going to be. From their reactions, you have to gauge if they really know anything. You listen very carefully. Got that?''

"I've got it. I could start now, if you want. This is when telemarketers usually hit.''

"Never mind the telemarketers. Go home and get a good night's sleep. You'll be more alert.''

She wondered why he didn't use Rochelle, if she was so good. He must have had a reason.

Or maybe he just didn't care.

Chapter Seven

By the time Lily reached home, Pat and Charlene had finished eating.

"We didn't know when you'd be here," Pat apologized, "so we went ahead."

"Donald called three times already," Charlene added.

Lily made herself a sandwich, and then returned his call.

He was losing patience. "I've been trying to get you. What happened?"

"Work. I'm sorry. It was an emergency."

"I hope that guy's paying you double overtime. Is he?"

"Well, not double, but I get paid for every hour."

"I keep telling you, Lily, you could do better. I'll see you in about twenty minutes."

He arrived with a carton of frozen yogurt, which they all shared. It was lemon flavor. Something about it stirred a memory that Lily could not pin down. A neutral memory, neither pleasant nor unpleasant. Her mind drifted, until Donald snapped his fingers in her face.

"How about taking a walk?"

Another walk. He never varied his routine, even to stop somewhere for a cup of cappuccino. Anything just a little different.

Pat saw them to the door. "Now watch yourself, young lady. Make sure you come home at a decent hour this time."

The door closed. Donald turned to Lily, his eyebrows a question mark. "What's she talking about? What was indecent about last night? It wasn't even ten o'clock."

"She's a kindergarten teacher," Lily explained. "That sort of thing comes naturally."

"I want to know what she meant."

There was no evading Donald. He was like a bull-dog.

"Okay. After you brought me home, I went for a walk." She pressed the elevator button a second time. Donald scowled. Repeated pressing didn't make it come faster.

"I don't understand," he said. "We already had a

walk. I brought you right to the door. I saw you go inside.''

She pushed the button again. ''Well, what happened was, after I got on the elevator, I started feeling claustrophobic. It was a nice night, so I went back outside.''

The car arrived and they stepped onto it.

''You never got claustrophobic in an elevator before,'' Donald said.

''I know, but sometimes I just like to walk around at night and think.''

''That's the worst thing you can do. If you're thinking, you're not alert for muggers.''

''Donald, are you going to spend your life bossing me around?''

''I care about you! I'm concerned.''

''You talk as if I'm a demented old lady.'' She hurried across the lobby, not wanting to hear his answer. Oscar swung the door open for them, nodding politely. She nodded back as though nothing had happened last night.

It wasn't Oscar's fault. She knew that. He could not have stopped the police. She only wished he hadn't seen her being hauled away.

Donald started toward the river.

''We went there yesterday,'' she said. ''Why don't we try something different for a change? How about Fifth Avenue?''

''What's there,'' he asked suspiciously, ''except

Central Park, and we aren't . . . I hope you didn't walk in the park at night!''

"Of course I didn't. I'm not suicidal.''

He cared. He said so. But he protected her as though she were an inferior creature who couldn't manage on her own. She wondered if he would have more respect for her once she got her law degree, even though he didn't think highly of lawyers.

She rested her hands on the rail above the riverbank and looked out at the water. Somewhere beyond those industrial lights of Queens, Mary Whelan dreamed of past and future love. If Lily could find Bobby Decatur and hand him over, gift wrapped, that would be a real accomplishment.

"What's the smile for?'' Donald asked.

"I was just thinking of our client who lives over there. The one with the high school sweetie. Wouldn't it be nice if I could bring them together and they lived happily ever after?''

"What's this guy like?''

"Bobby Decatur? How would I know? I haven't found him yet.''

"I mean the detective. What's he like?''

"I don't know him very well. He hasn't been around much. He's youngish. Grew up on Bleecker Street and he used to be a cop. I think he's in a relationship with some showgirl who works for him.''

"Lily, this doesn't sound like you. These are not your kind of people.''

"Excuse me?"

"Detectives. Showgirls."

She had known Donald for five years. She knew his attitudes, so why was she surprised? "I suppose you want me to quit the job and associate with 'my' kind of people, whatever that is."

"The magazine job was better," he said.

"Donald, the magazine doesn't exist anymore. The world changes, like it or not. Things happen. I can't go back to a job that doesn't exist."

A plane flew over them, drowning her out.

"Anyway," she went on, " 'editorial assistant' might sound important, but you're really just a gofer. In my present job—which by the way is only temporary, so you don't have to worry—at least I have some responsibilities. Tomorrow I get to entrap a guy over the phone. Someone who kidnapped his children. Don't you want me to have that kind of fun?"

"I want you to have whatever makes you happy." He tried to take her in his arms. They tripped over each other's feet and fell laughing onto a bench.

"I'm all for you going to law school, if that's what it takes." He kissed her ear. "If I could afford to help, I'd send you right now, so you don't have to take any more temp work. Maybe there's an opening at the hospital—"

He jumped up from the bench and dusted off his pants as two teenage boys approached. The boys glanced at them and walked on. She had thought at first that Donald was nervous. Some teenagers were predators. But he was only protecting his dignity.

Silently she thanked them for interrupting. Donald seemed to have forgotten his idea about finding work for her at the hospital.

The next morning, as she rode the subway to work mashed, buffeted, and clinging to a strap, she went over the telephone speech she had planned. It would be tricky, saying just enough to excite George Harding's interest but not to arouse his suspicion. There was a lot at stake if she messed up.

On her way from Fourteenth Street she stopped at a card shop and bought a map of Queens. There had to be someone in Rego Park who remembered the Decatur family and knew where they had gone. She could ring doorbells on Saturday while Donald was at work. In weather like this, she might not even have to ring. They would all be out washing their cars.

Al buzzed her into the office. "I was going to give you a key," he said.

"You did mention something about it."

He gave her four keys. One was for a burglar alarm, another for the outside door of heavy iron grillwork, which was kept open in the daytime. The inner door had two locks for extra security.

"Be sure you turn off the alarm before you touch anything else." He showed her where it was. Then he sat her down and checked his watch. "Okay, let's hear how you're going to do this."

"I never won a sweepstakes," she apologized. "I really don't know who would make this kind of call or what they'd say."

Another look at his watch. She had forgotten about Debbie Morrissey.

"If it makes you feel better," he said, "chances are, George Harding never did either. How's he going to know if you're following form? Make up something. Just remember to talk with authority. Don't waver or get self-conscious. Any phoniness will show right through."

He handed her the receiver, pressing a button to shut off the dial tone. She practiced with the first name on her list, a cousin of George Harding's in Corpus Christi, Texas.

"Hello, this is Lily Foster of the Circulation Management Sweepstakes. I'm calling for Mr. George Harding. We have some good news—"

"No, no," Al interrupted. "Don't say anything definite or you'll have everybody claiming to be George Harding. Just tell them it's an important message. And *listen*."

"What if somebody does claim to be George Harding? How will I know?"

"Then you get the address. Tell him you have to send a release form. Don't say anything about money. If he clams up, that could be a tip-off. Don't be too specific and don't press. All you want is a reaction, and it's going to be subtle. You'll have to stay on your toes.''

"If Rochelle is so good at this," Lily said, "how come you don't have her do it? She was looking for work."

"There are reasons. Okay, let's try it again."

She repeated her introduction. "I have an important message for Mr. George Harding. May I speak with him, please?"

"He's not here," said Al, playing the part of George's cousin. "What do you want to talk to him about?"

"Can you tell me when he'll be in? I need to discuss this personally."

Al shook his head. "Leave that off about talking to him personally, unless they back you into a corner. It's enough to scare a guy who's on the run."

They tried the dialogue once more and Al offered to take a message. He tapped the third button on the phone. She gave the number that was printed beside it.

"If that line rings," he said, "answer with your name. Don't mention me and don't give the company name. And by the way, he can call collect. Don't make a big point of it, just try to sound accommodating, but that way we'll have a record of where he's at."

They tried it several more times, stopping only for incoming calls. At last he was satisfied.

"There's other things we're going to try too," he said. "You were right to get his Social Security number. That's basic. Find out from the wife if he has other skills he could use to earn a living. I'll get hold of Motor Vehicles and see if he registered a car. He could have bought one if he had some money stashed away."

"Most private school teachers don't earn very much," Lily said.

"Thanks. If Motor Vehicles is negative, you're going to check every rental agency in the city. We'll follow up on the friend he was living with. He may know more than he lets on. Or he may know things he doesn't know he knows."

"This is exciting."

"It is? I hope you still think so when you're calling all those rental places."

After he left for his second try at the Morrissey girl, Lily started on her phone calls. George's mother, Amalie, who lived in Charlotte, was guarded. Lily felt sure she knew her son's whereabouts, but that he was not in the Virgin Islands.

"Why don't you give me a message?" Mrs. Harding suggested. "If he gets in touch with me, I can pass it along."

"Would you?" Lily gave her the number. "He can call me collect anytime during business hours."

The conversation left her feeling shaky. How could he help but guess that this was a way of tracking him down?

She tried another number. It was a private home in North Carolina. As soon as a woman answered with a child crying in the background, Lily hung up.

She hadn't expected this. She expected men friends, or George himself. Leaving a message was all right, but what if he got the same call from several different friends? It wouldn't take him long to figure out who had supplied the list of names.

Still, her boss had told her to do it, and he knew best. She called the other five numbers. Only one, in Arizona, answered. "Who?" said a male voice. "Oh, yeah, George. I think he lives in New York City."

"I was told he moved out west," Lily said.

"Who told you that?"

"At his former address they told me."

"Where did you say you're calling from?"

"This is the Circulation Management Sweepstakes in New York City. Please have Mr. Harding call me collect as soon as possible." She gave the number.

This might have been it. How could she tell? The man had asked a lot of questions for someone who claimed not to know where George was. At this rate, she would end up thinking everybody was harboring George.

She remembered the baby crying in North Carolina. One of the Harding children was only eighteen months old. That cry had sounded younger, but Lily was no expert on babies.

She answered two calls and was about to try North Carolina again when another call came in.

It was Al. "Just checking. I'm at my car phone, but don't use it unless you have to."

She brought him up to date. "It could have been anybody's baby. They all sound alike, but I got to thinking, what if it's his?"

"No, they don't all sound alike," he said. "They even cry different. See that tape machine on the desk? The thing with the suction cup, that's a telephone pickup. Stick it on the phone at the listening end, with a little spit to get it tight, and set it to record when you make your call. Then get the Harding woman over there and play it for her. But hurry up before the kid stops crying."

He was wrong. Except for the spit, this *was* exciting. She readied the tape and dialed the number.

That time, no one answered.

She had failed. To distract herself, she looked up Mary Whelan's old high school in the Queens directory. They had no current address for Bobby Decatur, and told her they wouldn't give it out if they did.

Lily thought fast. "Wait a minute! There is something you can help me with. I'm calling from Barberini Security." It sounded important, like a bank or the FBI. "Do you have a record of what college he attended?"

The person mumbled, but did not hang up. After a while, she announced, "Brooklyn College."

"Thank you very much. I appreciate this."

Lily found the number for Brooklyn College, but something needled her to try North Carolina again first.

Seven rings. She was about to give up when the ringing stopped. Quickly she set the dictaphone to record.

"H'llo," said a male voice. It didn't sound southern.

"Hello! How are you today? My name is Lily Foster, from the Circulation Management Sweepstakes. I'm calling for a Mr. George Harding. Are you Mr. Harding?"

"You're from what?"

Elated, she thought she heard a note of panic in his voice. She spoke soothingly, hoping he wouldn't hang up.

"We're the Circulation Management Sweepstakes. Mr. Harding's name was entered in one of our drawings. Is he there?"

"I don't know what you're talking about."

"Are you Mr. George Harding?"

"No, I'm not! What sort of drawing is this?"

"It's our annual seven-million-dollar sweepstakes. I can't give out any more information."

"I could take a message for him."

"Would you please? Just have him reverse the charges." Again she gave the number, and then called Susan.

"I'm not real sure about this," Lily said. "I need

some personal information. Very personal, that only your husband would know.''

''My *ex*-husband. Did you find him? Already?''

''That's the trouble. I can't tell. If it's not your husband, it might be somebody who knows where he is. They asked if he could get back to me. In case he does, I need to be sure it's him. What's his mother's maiden name, for instance?''

''McFee,'' said Susan. ''But it's possible his friends might know that. How about what he gave me for our first anniversary?''

''It shouldn't be anything that involves you, or he'll get suspicious. And it can't be anything a sweepstakes person wouldn't know. Which would include his mother's maiden name, come to think of it. Anyway, I recorded the conversation. I'd like you to hear it and tell me if you recognize the voice.''

''I'll try to get a break right now.''

Lily opened the Yellow Pages to Automobile Rental and Leasing. While she contemplated pages of listings, someone called from a jewelry wholesaler. ''We've noticed merchandise disappearing from our shipments. We think it may be some of the employees. Does Barberini handle that kind of thing?''

''As far as I know, he does.'' Lily chose a form for Employee Theft and took down the preliminary information.

Susan Harding arrived, taut and pale. ''I didn't think

you'd find him so soon. The police were trying. I know they were.''

''We may not have found him. I hope you can accept that.'' Lily played the tape for her.

Susan listened, her eyes widening. ''That's him.'' She clutched at her chest. *''That's him!''*

Chapter Eight

"Are you sure?" Lily asked. How could it be so easy?

"That's his voice! He's there! In Greensboro. What do we do now?" Susan began to cry.

Lily handed her the tissue box. "Now we leave it up to Mr. Barberini."

"What if George goes somewhere else in the meantime?"

It was a real possibility. "We'll do everything we can to keep that from happening. I know my boss feels strongly about cases like yours." At least he felt strongly about the Morrissey girl, and this was even worse.

Now that George had been placed, it no longer seemed necessary to call the rental agencies.

But what if Susan was mistaken? She might have believed it was George because she wanted it to be.

Lily called two agencies near where George had been living. It occurred to her that he might have rented using someone else's credit card. That would make more sense than allowing himself to be traced. Discouraged, she called Brooklyn College instead.

As she waited for them to look up Robert Decatur, the door buzzer rang. She covered the receiver and shouted, "Who is it?"

"Sergeant Muldoon, Miss Foster. We've got a few more questions for you."

"Ma'am?" said Brooklyn College. "The latest address we have is Valley Stream."

How could Muldoon have more questions? He had asked her everything twice.

"Just a minute, please," she called. "I'm on the phone."

In reply, he buzzed again. She managed to get Decatur's street address and thank the college before buzzing in the detective.

There were two of them, both huge. The other was a bald African-American who identified himself as George Washington.

"What's this 'Just a minute, please'?" demanded Muldoon, mimicking her voice.

"I'm sorry," Lily said. "I was on the phone getting some information. I couldn't cut her off."

"Lemme ask you something, Miss Foster. Do you wear perfume?"

"Perfume? I guess so, sometimes. Not to work, usually."

Muldoon grunted. Lily turned to his companion. "You must be the Washington I talked to yesterday about the pictures."

Muldoon said, "There were no pictures found in the victim's handbag, Miss Foster. Are you sure you didn't take them back?"

"I never saw them. I didn't think about the pictures when I found Mrs. Lanken on the floor. I was trying to revive her."

"You never saw the pictures after she took them?"

"I never saw them at all. She stamped on my foot and knocked me down. Before I could get up, she grabbed them out of the file drawer. I can't even be sure it was her pictures she took, except there aren't any in her file now. I looked there after I found out her name."

A mocking smile twitched at Washington's mouth. "She knocked you down? That little old lady?"

"She stamped on my foot," Lily repeated, and held it out so they could see the bandage. "With a sharp heel. Before I caught my breath, she pushed me. She's a wiry old thing."

Washington's face showed no expression. Muldoon

moved closer, planting his hands on her desk. She drew back from the rank smell of sweat.

"Let me get this straight, Miss Foster. You didn't want her to have the pictures, right?"

"I didn't care if she had the pictures. All I tried to do was stop her from going through the files. They're full of people's secrets. How did I know she wasn't a blackmailer? She wouldn't tell me who she was."

"She says she told you everything you asked."

"Well, that's not true. But I'm glad she's conscious and talking."

"Mind if we have a look at Mrs. Lanken's file?"

Lily hesitated. They had looked all over the place on Wednesday, but not specifically at Mrs. Lanken's file.

"You're wondering if we need a search warrant," Muldoon guessed. "Miss Foster, this office was the scene of a crime. We don't need a warrant. But it so happens we have one here, which we're going to use later." He waved a folded paper at her.

"Mrs. Lanken's file," she told them, pointing toward the cabinet, "is in the top drawer, under Lanken. They're in alphabetical order."

The two men glared at her. She hadn't meant to sound sarcastic. She was only trying to be helpful.

They took out the folder and looked through it, then handed it back to Lily for refiling.

"No pictures anywhere," Muldoon said. "And no diamond bracelet. Kinda makes you wonder what happened." He pulled out a chair and sat down. "Tell me, Miss Foster. How's business?"

"Excuse me?"

"This business. Barberini whatever it is. How's he doing financially?"

"I have no idea. This is only my third day here, and I'm just filling in. He seems to keep pretty busy."

"Money coming in okay?"

"I wouldn't know. It's not only that I'm new, he's out most of the time. I never really talked to him, except the other night. After that questioning. He drove me home."

"He didn't talk about money?"

"No, he talked about growing up on Bleecker Street and how his mother likes to cook." He hadn't said much at all. She knew very little of Al.

"I don't even know where he lives," she said. "Or how he lives. So I'm afraid I can't answer your question."

They couldn't suspect *Al*. That was ridiculous. Besides, he had been out on surveillance when Lanken was attacked.

"Now according to an earlier statement, you told this other girl, Roxanne Pulver, that Lanken was coming over."

"Rochelle. I told her because I wanted her advice, but she didn't give me any. She was gone long before Mrs. Lanken got here, and she didn't come back in. I would have seen her."

"What do you know about the super, José Rodriguez?"

"I don't know anything about him. Al says he wouldn't have done it."

"Oh, Al would be an authority on that? Did he happen to mention how much Rodriguez drops on the horses?"

She answered distantly, "He didn't say anything about horses. But he knows José better than I do. I don't know why you're asking me all this. Until Wednesday, I never even heard of these people."

"You were here when it happened, Miss Foster. You're the only one who was."

"Except for the person who tried to strangle Mrs. Lanken," Lily pointed out.

"Except for that person," Muldoon agreed, with forced amiability. "I'm asking you, Miss Foster, because only these people and yourself had access to this place."

"Al has some other part-timers," she told him. "I don't know how many or who they are."

"They don't have keys." Muldoon's smirk became broader, flashing a silver filling. He gave Washington a nudge. "Let's go. Miss Foster, how do we get to the super's apartment?"

"I don't know where he lives," said Lily.

"Upstairs, Miss Foster. This is the first floor, right? Or is it the basement?"

"I think you'll have to go outside, then. I don't know of any stairway from here."

She watched them leave and felt as though she were feeding José to the lions. But what could she have done?

It must have been the same for Oscar, the doorman at her building. He had even tried to warn her with his eyes.

Valley Stream was not in the Queens directory. She checked her map and discovered it was over the line in Nassau County.

On a shelf in the middle room there were phone books for the whole tri-state area. Al was well prepared, and she could see why. Much of his business was done on the phone.

While she pored through the book, José came in. His round face was careworn, drooping at the mouth. His liquid eyes accused her.

"Miss," he began in a soft wheeze. "I don't know your name. You don't know my name."

"Yes, I do," she said. "You're Mr. Rodriguez. I'm sorry. They had a search warrant."

"What do you tell them about me?"

"Absolutely nothing. I don't know anything about you."

"What do you tell them that they come and look in my apartment? They open the drawers. They make a big mess."

"I didn't tell them anything, Mr. Rodriguez. That's

the truth. All I said was that Mr. Barberini doesn't believe you would do a thing like that. Really, that was it. I don't believe you would either," she added in self-defense.

"Then why do they come and pull out everything?"

"They said"—she counted on her fingers—"that you, I, Mr. Barberini, and Rochelle Pulver are the only ones who could have gotten in here that day. They're probably searching all of us. In fact, the night it happened, they took me downtown for questioning."

He was silent, but no less unhappy. Lily had visions of the police ransacking her own apartment, looking for a diamond bracelet, with Pat and Charlene standing by in shock.

"Obviously," she said, "somebody else must have gotten in here. I don't know who or how."

"I don't let nobody in," he insisted.

"A determined person could probably manage no matter what you do. Maybe they climbed over the back fence."

"I don't let nobody in. I don't hurt no old ladies." He turned and shuffled out.

They ought to sue Mrs. Lanken, Lily thought, for wearing a diamond bracelet and getting them all in trouble. It was for people like José that she wanted to be a lawyer.

Returning to the phone book, she found Decatur, Robert and Lisa, in Valley Stream.

So he was married. To verify it, Lily dialed the number.

She was answered by an elderly quaver. His mother! Mary Whelan still had a chance.

"Mrs. Decatur?" Lily said. "I'm calling from—"

"Mrs. Decatur's not in," said the voice. "This is the baby-sitter."

"Oh. Well, actually it's Mr. Decatur I'm looking for. Can you tell me how to reach him? I'm calling from the Second National Bank."

"*Doctor* Decatur," said the voice with a touch of pride, "is in his shop."

"I see. What shop is that?"

"His eyeglasses shop! Bobbyvision. He's an optometrist."

The shop was in Brooklyn. Lily got the number and dialed it.

She had to wait until Bobby was finished with a customer. She stared hard at the telephone, willing it not to ring. Willing Al to stay away. They offered to have Bobby call her, but people never called back right away. It could be days.

Finally he answered, sounding rushed. "Doctor Decatur here."

"Oh, yes," Lily said. "I'm with a security company in Manhattan."

"I don't need a security system. I already have one."

"No, wait. I'm not trying to sell anything. We're a

private detective firm. We were hired by someone to look you up.''

"Huh? She knows where I am. I pay my child support. What's her beef this time?''

So that explained the babysitter. He was on his second family, probably a young wife and new young children.

"Dr. Decatur, this has nothing to do with that. It's someone you knew back in high school. She's divorced now and is trying to get in touch with you. Mary Whelan.''

"I don't know any . . . Oh, her. What does she want?''

"Since apparently you're happily married, I guess it's out of the question. She wanted to renew your acquaintance.''

"What for? Listen, whoever you are, I *am* happily married. I don't want anything to do with that. What was it, twenty-five years ago? What in blazes does she have to pop up again for?''

A motion outside the window caught her eye. It was Al. He came in, rumpled and wearing the baseball cap askew, and stood listening.

Lily dropped her voice. "It was just an idea she had. But if you're not interested—''

"I'll say I'm not interested,'' fumed the doctor. "How did you find me?''

"Through the usual channels, sir.''

"Well, listen. You'd better tell that woman to leave

me alone. If I hear from her even once, I'm going to get an order of protection. Who did you say you are?''

"I didn't say, but you don't need to worry." Trying to ignore Al's presence, she buried her mouth in the receiver. "We haven't passed along any information. I'll tell her you moved to Australia."

"Tell her I died. But keep her away from me. Is that understood? I don't want any phone calls. I don't want her coming in for an eye exam. I don't want the phone ringing, and when I answer it, nobody's there. Do you know what I mean? I don't want that."

"Usually, when that happens, it's a wrong number," Lily said. "I promise you, she has no idea where you are and we'll keep it that way. You have my word. And thanks for your time."

Al hadn't missed anything. "What was that all about?"

"Oh, just some eye doctor."

"You found the guy, right? Now you see why I don't like those cases?"

"Yes, I understand. But he *might* have wanted to see her."

"If I get a lawsuit on my hands—"

"You won't. He doesn't know who we are and he didn't seem to care much."

"Lily, finding a lost kid is legitimate. Or a lost parent or some other relative, that's legitimate. But a lover from thirty years back . . . ''

"Sometimes people really do want to get together," she insisted. "Did you find Debbie Morrissey?"

"Yeah, we got her. She went home with her dad. If they get some family counseling, it might work out. How did you track this guy?"

"Bobby Decatur? I asked his high school where he went to college, then I asked his college. It was really easy."

"Sometimes it is." He folded his arms, still disapproving. "What else happened today?"

"The police came. They had more questions and they searched José's apartment. He was very upset. And they looked in Mrs. Lanken's file to see if the pictures were there. They said she didn't have them after the attack. But I saw her take them and put them in her purse."

"Interesting. Anything else?"

"Yes. I called that number again. . . ."

She stopped to answer the ringing phone. A gentle voice asked, "Is this the detective's office?"

"Yes, it is. May I help you?"

"I'm looking for someone. . . ."

It was exactly how Mary Whelan had begun. Al stood watching and listening.

"Miss," Lily said, "could I take your number and call you back in a few minutes?"

The woman's name was Elissa Brock. Lily wrote down the number and then told Al about her call to North Carolina.

"I got a man this time and I taped it. Susan Harding said it's her husband. In Greensboro. She didn't have any doubt."

"Greensboro, huh? Do you have the address?"

"Yes. It's one of his friends."

She played the tape so Al could hear it, and copied the address and phone number for him. "Do you want me to keep on with the rental agencies?"

"Let's check this out first. You're doing okay, Lily. I might need you on this one. But stay away from those lost lovers."

Chapter Nine

Al went into his office and closed the door. He needed to make his phone calls undisturbed. So did Lily. She dialed the number Mrs. Brock had given her.

"It's someone I lost a long time ago," Brock began.

"Excuse me," Lily interrupted. "Is this by any chance an old boyfriend?"

There was a moment of hesitation.

"He was more than a boyfriend. He was my life. We wanted to marry, but my father didn't approve. They took me away to California and I lost touch with James. I never forgot him. We loved each other so much."

Except for a few differences, it could have been Mary Whelan. "I'm awfully sorry, Mrs. Brock. We don't usually take that kind of case. Very often the person being looked for has gone on and made a life for himself, and he may not want to be found.''

"But James loved me! I only want to see if he still does. Couldn't you please help me? Please?''

The soft, cultured pleading was more than Lily could bear.

"I'm only a secretary,'' she explained. "It's my boss who makes the decisions. We just had a bad experience with something like this.'' Which reminded her that she hadn't yet called Mary Whelan to break the news.

"Oh, no!'' cried Mrs. Brock. "I wouldn't give you any trouble. I certainly don't want to make trouble for James.''

It was exactly what Whelan had said.

"I've already tried, you see,'' she went on. "I hired another detective to look for James. He came back and told me James had died. I couldn't believe it.''

"Sometimes it's hard to accept that,'' Lily agreed.

"No, you don't understand. I know he's alive. I can sense it. We always had this feeling between us.''

"Well, uh—''

"Please? You probably think I'm crazy, believing he's alive, but I really do. I think they must have found the wrong James Dembrovsky. I'd like you to set it right, if you can. There won't be any problem about money. My husband left me quite well off.''

"You're a widow?''

"Yes. I had a good marriage and I was a good wife, but I missed James. He was my soulmate. I should say he still is. Do you understand what I mean?"

"I think so. Why don't you give me the information?" And quickly, before Al opened his door. "I'll get back to you next week."

James Dembrovsky would have been forty-nine. He and Elissa had grown up together in Greenwich Village, when she was Elissa Mahon. James's father was a janitor, which didn't meet the standards of Elissa's parents.

"I knew he could make something of himself. He had such a beautiful soul, but my parents were just prejudiced. They took me to California and didn't leave any forwarding address. For three years they watched over me. They screened all my mail and phone calls. Then I married Calvin Brock. He was a good man. Nothing can take that away. We had a boy and a girl, both grown now. After Calvin passed on I came back to Greenwich Village. I always considered it home, but maybe that's because of James."

"I'll do what I can, Mrs. Brock."

There was a tightness in Lily's throat. A yearning. For what, she didn't know. Someone else's great love? Her own great love? Maybe not everybody had a James Dembrovsky. Their romance sounded like something out of Shakespeare.

Maybe James wasn't really so remarkable. Elissa

could have been idealizing, especially after so many years.

In any case, it was time to call Mary Whelan. Lily dreaded it.

She had thought she would tell the truth. But perhaps that was a bad idea with someone so obsessed. If Whelan knew Bobby was in the area, she might not give up easily. While the phone rang, Lily concocted a story. It was melodramatic but foolproof.

Mary greeted her with excitement. "Did you find him?"

"Not exactly." It was shocking how easily people could lie when they had to. "I found out *about* him. It seems he ran into a problem some years ago. The place where he worked, a clothing factory, had a run-in with the Mob. Mr. Decatur was called to testify, and there were death threats. They had to put him in the Witness Protection Program."

"What does that mean?"

"It means he's someone else now. He had to assume a new identity, move somewhere else, and there's no way to trace him. Only the FBI knows where he is, and they never tell. Of course his wife and children went with him."

"Bobby's . . . gone?"

"Very much so. I'm sorry, Miss Whelan. But I'm sure there's someone out there waiting to meet you. Just relax and keep an open mind. It might not be the person you expect."

Lily was surprised at her own wisdom. She sat mulling it over as she reached for the warbling telephone.

It was Donald. "They called a staff meeting tonight. I don't know how late it's going to run. I have to be at work by seven in the morning, so let's just forget it this time, shall we?"

"That's fine, Donald. Don't worry about me."

"You go right home and stay there, Lily. Don't take any walks."

"I'll do my nails," she promised.

Al came out of his office, minus the baseball cap. He had changed his shirt and combed his hair. "You doing anything for dinner tonight?"

"Me? No, I was going to go home and . . . polish my nails."

"They look okay. How about helping me celebrate the Morrissey case? Just give me a few minutes. I'm waiting to hear from Greensboro."

Lily was dumbfounded. He couldn't be hitting on her! No, it was just a friendly invitation, because it was Friday. They had weathered three days together, as well as a case of attempted murder.

Inspired, she took out Mrs. Lanken's file and looked through it while she waited for him.

Lanken was sixty-eight. Born and raised in Bronxville, New York. Barnard College. It was too bad they hadn't sent her to charm school.

Lily found a note referring to some photos taken in March by R.P. Could that be Rochelle? It was no wonder she had wanted to send flowers, if she was working on the case.

A newspaper clipping described Barry Lanken's latest project, a series of children's classics. An article from a trade paper recounted his efforts at finding sponsors. He had a children's clothing manufacturer lined up. A breakfast food company. A bubble bath product. All wholesome and child-related.

His problem began to take shape. If the wife made a stink about marital infidelity, some or all of those sponsors might pull out. With that much on the line, he might have felt driven to silence her.

Possibly he had hired someone to do it for him. But the fact remained, no one had come through the front door that afternoon.

It all went back to José. Muldoon had said he was fond of the horses, and José could get in and out without passing Lily. He might have been so deeply in debt that he took on an extra job.

José, with those wounded eyes and the round, indignant face. Could it have been an act?

Lily read on to the crux of the case, Barry Lanken's girlfriend. She was a television actress named Sharon May. Twenty-six years old. There was a brief description, but not enough to portray a recognizable person. It was too bad Mrs. Lanken had taken all the pictures.

She tried the phone book. No Sharon May was listed. She checked all five boroughs, and then turned to *How to Find Out Anything about Anybody*.

Actors' unions! She hadn't thought of that. The most likely would be the Screen Actors' Guild and AFTRA, the American Federation of Television and Radio Artists.

"Ready?" said Al. "What are you looking up this time?"

She jumped. She hadn't known he was there. "I was just checking something. This book is fascinating."

She put away the folder, glad he hadn't seen it, while he set the answering machine.

"Do you always celebrate when you solve a case?" she asked as they left the office.

"That's just an excuse. I eat out all the time, but usually alone. It's nice to have company."

"Why alone? Don't you have a girlfriend?"

"Not at the moment."

"What about Rochelle?"

"Rochelle!" He stopped at a red light. "Why Rochelle?"

"She kind of implied there was something going on. Or maybe I misunderstood."

"You must have. There's nothing going on."

At the next block, they entered a doorway with a green canopy over it. ERNESTO'S it said in script on the canopy.

Ernesto's had two dining rooms. The one in back was a glass-enclosed garden with dividers of white latticework and the cool, moist smell of growing plants.

The ivy on the latticework was real. So were the hanging baskets and the potted shrubs.

The waiter showed them to a table for four. Instead of sitting across from her, Al took the chair next to hers.

"This is beautiful," Lily said. "What do they do at night when there's no sun shining in?"

"They turn on the lights. They've got them on now. Would you like something to drink?"

"If you're having it."

He shook his head. "Not me. I don't drink, even wine. But you go ahead."

"Maybe I'll have Perrier." She had never drunk Perrier in her life. It seemed an affectation, but she didn't want to order wine if he was going to be so principled.

"What's that like?" he asked when it arrived.

"Try it." She offered him the glass.

He took a cautious sip. "Bubbly water."

"That's exactly what it is." She moved it into a patch of light on the tablecloth and watched the bubbles explode. "Like diamonds . . . I wish I hadn't said that, it reminds me of Mrs. Lanken. And that reminds me, a call came in from some jewelry company this afternoon. They think their employees are stealing. I assume you handle those things, since you have a form for it."

"Employee theft is most of my business," he said. "It's not as interesting as finding missing kids, but it's good, solid income. Employers are willing to pay."

"Is that what the message was about on Wednesday? Was that employee theft?"

"What message?"

"The one I put on your desk." A feeling of dread crawled down her spine. "About the warehouse."

"What warehouse?"

"Didn't you see it? My first day of work. Something about a warehouse at seven o'clock on Friday. They said you'd know."

"You put it on my desk? When?"

"On Wednesday. You were out. I put it right on top of your desk. I'm sorry. I didn't think about it."

He looked at his watch. "Why didn't you tell me?"

"I thought you got it. And then that thing happened with Mrs. Lanken—"

He flung ten dollars onto the table and bolted from the restaurant. She sat for a moment, trying to recover, and then gathered up her purse.

The waiter hurried over. Lily said, "He had to leave. I'm sorry. That's for your trouble." She pointed to the money. They hadn't ordered yet, except for the Perrier.

She reached the street in time to see Al climb into a taxi. Calling, she ran toward him. She would offer to go and help. Anything to atone.

He pulled the door closed and the taxi drove off.

Chapter Ten

A subway train rattled in the distance. She was on the platform and didn't know how she had gotten there.

She *had* given him the message. He would never believe her. She remembered Rochelle sitting at his desk making a phone call. Maybe she had seen it. Maybe those busy hands had managed to bury it. Lily thought of going back to the office, checking his desk, but the train came at that moment and she boarded it.

She hoped her roommates would be out. It was Friday night. Pat had a steady boyfriend who worked at the Bronx Zoo. She had met him there on a field trip with her class. Charlene had an on-again, off-again relationship with someone in her office.

And now it was off again. Lily heard the television as soon as she opened the door.

Charlene was on the couch, eating tortilla chips and salsa. "Hi! I wondered where you were."

"That's not dinner, is it?" Lily asked.

"I didn't feel like cooking just for me. Have some."

Lily took a chip without the salsa. She wasn't hungry.

Charlene seemed content. "So tell me what exciting things happened today."

"Nothing much. He got the runaway girl. I found the high school sweetie, but he's married and didn't want anything to do with our client. Then we got another case just like it . . . "

What would she do about Elissa Brock? Al didn't want the case and Lily had promised to call her back. She didn't even have Brock's phone number.

"There's butterscotch ice cream in the freezer," Charlene said.

"You wouldn't."

"I needed it. But after I got in the checkout line and it was too late to take it back, I started thinking how I always comfort myself with food. I'll end up a blimp and nobody will love me. You're so lucky to have Donald *and* a figure."

"I'm not lucky. There's nothing good about my life right now. Don't ask."

They sat in silence, eating chips and ice cream and

watching an Eddie Murphy picture. At ten o'clock Lily went to bed.

The telephone woke her. Amber sunlight slanted through the venetian blind. It was barely dawn. Charlene, who shared the room, groaned and turned over.

Maybe it was Donald. That would be better than a family emergency, which was the first thing that occurred to her.

"Is this Lily?"

At the sound of Al's voice, she sat up.

He went on without waiting. "Can you pack and be ready in an hour? Just overnight is all you'll need."

"Pack?"

"Sorry I woke you. Sorry to ruin your weekend. We're going to North Carolina. I'll pick you up in an hour. Try to be down at the curb. I know it's not much time."

"Okay." She put back the phone, wondering if it had really happened.

"What was that?" asked Charlene.

"My boss. He's picking me up in an hour."

"Oh, nice. But what about Donald? Lily, I have to warn you, an office romance is not the best way to go."

"It has nothing to do with romance." Lily hurried into the shower.

When she came out, Charlene was sitting up in bed.

"He called again. He said to bring your driver's license."

"I always have my driver's license." Lily reached up to the top closet shelf and brought down her carryon bag. A change of clothes. A nightgown. It was full summer, and in North Carolina it would be hot and humid.

Charlene watched her. "Excuse me for being nosy, but what's going on?"

"I think we're going to kidnap some children. I mean, get them back. They're already kidnapped."

"You have such a fun job." Charlene worked in a corporate office. It paid well, but was unexciting. "You said he's looking for somebody permanent. How come you don't apply?"

Lily winced, remembering last night. "I figured he had my résumé, and if he wanted me, he'd say so."

"Wrong! He probably thought if you wanted the job, *you'd* say so. You have to push for those things. Don't take anything for granted."

"Donald wants me to look for something better," Lily said. "Do you have a travel-size tube of toothpaste I could borrow?"

Charlene supplied toothpaste and shampoo. Lily ended up with more than one outfit, not knowing what was appropriate for retrieving kidnapped children.

She was getting a headache. Either it was stress, or there hadn't been time for coffee. She took an aspirin and went down to the curb.

Al arrived a minute later. "We might not have to stay over," he said as she got in beside him, "but it doesn't hurt to go prepared."

He hadn't said a word about the missing memo. She brought it up herself. "I'm sorry about last night."

"It's okay. Probably not your fault."

It *wasn't* her fault. She might even have remembered to tell him, if it hadn't been for Mrs. Lanken. "Maybe it got lost when the police were searching."

"Forget it," he said. "Everything worked out. Better late than never."

They hurtled down Second Avenue, keeping ahead of the staggered traffic lights. It was still early and there was not much traffic.

"We'll go back to Ernesto's sometime and do it right," he added. "That sounds like a song. 'Back to Sorrento.' You ever been there? Italy?"

"Yes. The summer I finished college I went to Europe. That was before I thought of saving for law school. I took a package tour because it's cheaper, but someday I'd like to do it on my own."

He turned onto the Queensborough Bridge. "When did you decide on law school?"

"That was quite recent. In college I planned to be a lab technician and work with Donald, but I didn't do that well in science. How come you're bringing me along on this trip?"

"I need someone George Harding doesn't know, so it can't be his wife. And in case we have to stay overnight I want a woman there to help with the kids, especially the girl.''

"When you went after Debbie Morrissey, you said her father had to be there so they wouldn't call it kidnapping.''

"That's right. But what we're going now is legal. George Harding's the lawbreaker.''

"Do you mean we'll actually go in there and—''

"No, the local police are going in there. We'll pave the way, is all, and then we'll bring the kids home.''

He turned in at LaGuardia Airport, where tickets waited for them at the counter. The plane had already begun boarding.

Their seats were in a row of three on the side. He put her next to the window and took the aisle seat, leaving an empty one between them. "I don't think the plane is going to be full,'' he said, lifting her bag to store it in an overhead bin.

The reality of what was happening had still not caught up with her. He had to remind her to fasten her seat belt. "This is going to take a little while. Do you want a magazine?''

"No, thanks. I brought a book.'' It was in her carryon, up in the bin. She stared out at the airport, at the luggage tram and the mechanics scurrying back and forth. It was all a weird dream.

A last-minute passenger came down the aisle accompanied by a flight attendant. They stopped next to Al, who unfastened his belt and moved into the middle seat. Lily pulled in her elbows and squeezed herself together.

He said, "Sorry I'm not the medical student."

"Oh, no, it's not that. It's just that I feel so bad about last night."

"Will you drop it? You didn't do anything wrong. I was upset, that's all, and I'm sorry. You were new that day and the whole place was crazy with the Lanken thing and the cops all over."

"It wasn't only the police. Rochelle made a phone call from your desk. It might have gotten pushed under something."

Al had nothing to say about that. Lily remembered Rochelle's proprietary manner. "Why didn't you bring her on this trip? She knows more than I do."

"Rochelle has an audition this afternoon. That's more important to her."

"Is that why you didn't get her to make those phone calls? You said she's good. I could have messed up and lost George Harding forever."

He took a breath and let it out. The plane's engines roared. "I don't usually discuss my employees with each other," he said into her ear. "But if it makes you feel better, since you're so down this morning, she may be good at playing a part, but the real trick is to listen. I told you that. Rochelle is too self-involved to do a good job of picking up on other people. I get the feeling you're more sensitive. Intuitive."

The engine sound grew louder. A flight attendant walked by, checking to see that all belts were fastened.

"Thank you," Lily said.

"Don't thank me," Al replied. "That's just the way it is. Maybe someday you'll make a good investigator."

The plane began to taxi. He leaned toward her again. "What did the police say yesterday?"

"They said only four people had access to the building. You, me, Rochelle, and José. They think it had to be one of us. They asked how your business is doing."

His face remained close to her ear. He said nothing. She turned to see what was happening.

His eyes had gold flecks. She had always thought they were pure brown. His scar was a white line. She could feel his breath on her cheek.

"That's crazy," he said. "Lanken's my bread and butter, some of it."

"I told them you seem pretty busy. And Rochelle wasn't even there. In fact, only I was. Somebody must have come through the back. You said he'd have to climb over that fence. Well, maybe he did."

"Maybe," he agreed, "but it would take some planning. First they'd have to see Lanken go in. A stranger on the street wouldn't know what part of the building she was going to. They'd have to gain access through some other building, and all of them are locked. Then they'd have to get in through our back door and know they could reach Lanken without being seen. How is your random mugger going to do all that?''

Lily felt chilled. It did sound more like a hit than a mugging.

''I guess that leaves me,'' she said, as the plane lurched forward on its takeoff roll. ''Or maybe José.''

''I guess it leaves the police with a lot of work to do.'' He settled back. Lily watched the earth race by and felt a bump as they left it and rose into the air.

''I hate takeoffs,'' she said. ''I always get queasy when we're tilted like this, but after we straighten out it's okay.''

He took her hand and held it on the armrest between them. ''Does this help?''

Strangely, it did, even though he wasn't Donald. She wondered what Donald would have done. Would he hold her hand to reassure her?

''I think you have more bedside manner than my fiancé,'' she said.

''A lot of doctors don't have much bedside manner,'' Al replied.

''I don't think José did it. Or maybe I don't want to think so. And I know I didn't.''

''That leaves me and Rochelle,'' he said.

''Rochelle and me.''

At his puzzled frown, she explained, ''That's the way you're supposed to say it. You put the other person first.''

"Okay, Penn State." His hand relaxed, letting go of hers.

"I learned that in grade school, not college," she said. "I'm sorry. It's my years on the magazine. And I wasn't even an editor."

"Better than me. I'm just an uneducated street kid from Little Italy."

"No, you're not." She let 'better than me' pass.

"I didn't go to college," he said.

"I think it's what you do with yourself that counts, what sort of person you are, not where you went to school." She was surprised to find her hand tightening again on his.

"Still scared?" he asked.

"Until we stop climbing. I'm not really scared. Just unnerved."

"You even have a fancy vocabulary to go with your degree, Penn State. Is that how you're going to talk to the other doctors' wives?"

"Do you know you've just given me the most dismal picture of my future. Sitting around talking to other doctors' wives. About what? The hospital auxiliary? That's my mother-in-law's big thing. I mean my future mother-in-law. I can even see the traditional living room with the brocaded furniture and silver tea service."

"Is that what you want?"

"I want to be a lawyer and *do* something. When I saw José's sad eyes . . . That's what I want to do. Help people who don't know how to help themselves. And I was one of them that night they dragged me in for questioning. I know what it's like.''

"Wow. You're going to be a public defender.'' He smiled. "You know, a lot of people who get in trouble really are guilty. But you're right, they deserve their day in court.''

"I don't know if I could defend a guilty person.''

His hand broke free again. She hadn't realized how tightly she was holding it.

"What kind of lawyer are you going to be if you won't defend guilty people?'' he asked. "A good defense lawyer does the best they can whether the client's guilty or innocent.''

"The best *he* can. Or she. 'Defense lawyer' is singular, so you have to use a singular pronoun.''

" 'They' covers both,'' he insisted. "And stop correcting me. With you around, I'll be submitting the most literary reports you ever saw to my clients.''

"The most literary reports to my clients that you ever saw.''

"That's just as bad.''

He wanted her to stay! If she took Charlene's advice, maybe she could work with him for a whole year— and then go off to the brocaded living room with the silver tea service.

But that would come later, when Donald was a full-fledged doctor. As an intern and wife they would probably have a small apartment furnished in cute modern.

They would get together with other intern families to talk about operations and rotations and hospital personnel and bemoan the ghastly hours. She wondered where they would be for that year. What if it was far away from any law school? What if she didn't get into law school?

How could she defend someone who she knew had done something horrible?

"What are you having?" asked Al.

She looked up to see the drink cart at the seat in front of theirs. "Coffee, please."

He ordered two. She asked, "Don't you ever drink? How come?" Maybe he was a recovering alcoholic and she should mind her own business.

"Because of something that happened once," he said. "Years ago."

"To you?"

"More to somebody else. I see you don't go in much for the hard stuff either."

She would never touch another Bloody Mary as long as she lived.

Again her efforts to find out more about him had failed. She turned instead to the project at hand. "How are we going to do this, exactly?"

"We're going to play it by ear," he said. "And we're not going to talk about it where people can hear us."

She didn't think anyone could hear over the engine

noise. But they always did when you least wanted them to.

She looked down at the ground. She supposed it was New Jersey. They were high enough now so the details were lost.

"You told me you quit being a cop," she said, "and there were reasons. Did you get hurt?"

He seemed not to hear her. She really was being inquisitive.

Then he said, "I was on the force six years. Joined when I was nineteen. I was this straight-arrow kid who thought I could make a difference. Like you with your law school."

"Do you think it's amusing? My boyfriend does. That's the word he used."

"Amusing, no. Maybe a little naive."

"What happened to change your mind about police work?"

"You're a determined lady, aren't you? I didn't change my mind about police work. Only about me. After I made detective, I was assigned to narcotics. You know that's a violent world."

"Yes, I know."

"My partner and I got into a shoot-out. A twelve-year-old kid was killed. I don't know whose shot it was, and I don't want to know. But a twelve-year-old is a *kid*."

"Yes, but some of them—"

"I know. That's what they said. The kid was dealing, he was armed and part of a gang. It was them or us. That might have been true. In New York, there are some pretty vicious twelve-year-olds. He was small and skinny and wore big, round glasses. A cute-looking kid. Father was gone. His mom worked as a nurse's aid to support him. People blame the parents, but what was she supposed to do, go on welfare? At least she was trying. He was her only child.''

"Oh, Al."

"Then the media got in and there was an investigation. A lot of stonewalling and cover-up. That was what I couldn't take. So maybe the kid was innocent. They should have been able to deal with the truth, whatever it was.''

"Most people aren't real good at admitting their mistakes," Lily said.

"Yes, and I think it's a sign of weakness. A departmental cover-up is a sign of departmental weakness.''

"So then you opened your own shop?''

"I didn't know what else to do. I'd been a police detective for three years so I qualified for a license.''

All that, and he had been only a year older than she was now.

"You seem to do pretty well as an investigator.''

"I get by.''

"That's what I told Muldoon.''

She looked down at New Jersey, or perhaps Pennsylvania, and wondered what Muldoon was coming up with.

Who would know that Mrs. Lanken would probably head for the bathroom? Al knew. Undoubtedly Mr. Lanken did, and he would share it with whomever he hired. It would be a good place for an ambush.

"I can see why Muldoon thinks I must have done it," she said. "There just wasn't anybody else, except José. He's the only one who could reach the back through that garbage gate. But even then, how did they get into the bathroom? Or maybe they were already there. Behind the shower curtain. It's opaque, isn't it?"

"They could have hit her when she came out," Al suggested. "She was struck on the head before they strangled her."

"I didn't know that. But unless she backed out, she'd have been facing them. She'd remember seeing them."

"Not necessarily. Usually with a trauma like that, people forget what happened just before as well as after."

"They couldn't count on it, could they? Whoever did it."

"They didn't mean for her to live."

The statement nudged at Lily's mind. Something was there, but she couldn't get hold of it. She rested against the window and fell asleep.

Awhile later she woke to see North Carolina coming up to meet them. They shuffled off the plane and Al rented a car, listing them both as drivers. His first stop was the police station, where the day's plans were coordinated.

"This isn't going to be easy," he told Lily. "The kids aren't in school yet. In fact, they aren't even visible. A man who might have been Harding, except he had a beard, was seen going in and out of the house, but there's no sign of the kids."

"He *must* have them! Unless he shipped them somewhere else."

"Chances are he does, but he's keeping them hidden. They may not even be in that house."

"I heard a baby crying," Lily said.

"The people who live there have a baby of their own."

"Do you mean this might all be a mistake?"

"That's what we need to find out. And you're the one who's going to do it. You'll have to get into that house."

Chapter Eleven

"**M**e?"

"You," Al repeated.

"But how? What if they find me out?" She saw herself held prisoner with a shotgun.

"We'll be right behind you," he promised. "Hidden, it goes without saying. You'll have to play a part. You've got to be convincing and innocent so they'll let you into the house."

"I wish Rochelle were here."

"Don't waste yourself wishing. This is the way it is, and you'd better listen carefully."

They briefed her on what she had to do. She was to drive the rented car while Al and several officers rode in a closed van. The police wore T-shirts and jeans and carried orange pylons, ostensibly for working on the street. They would be across from the house.

"If the children are there," Al instructed her, "when you get back in your car, roll down the window on the street side."

The windows were power operated. She would have to turn on the engine and press a button. She experimented to be sure she had the right one.

A few minutes after the van had parked, she drove down the street and stopped in front of the house. She felt a ringing in her ears. Her hands left damp marks on the padded steering wheel. She was not an actress. Not Rochelle. What if she made a mistake and blew the whole thing?

I can do it, she told herself. It was she, not Rochelle, who had found this man. It was she who had listened when she talked to him.

Maybe Susan's identification was wrong. A voice could be distorted on tape.

She opened the map of Greensboro they had given her and pretended to study it, regretting that she had turned off the engine. Already she was suffocating in southern heat. She reached for the window button without thinking.

Good thing the engine was off. If not, she would have rolled down the window too soon. Before she even got into the house.

It was pleasant and quiet in the early afternoon. Shade trees lined both sides of the street. She should have parked under one, but again she hadn't been thinking.

She opened her door and got out, remembering to look around, studying the numbers. Her target house was wood frame, painted a lime green with brown shutters. A peculiar combination, but cool. Noting its number, thirty-seven, she started up the walk.

Her black sleeveless blouse was already drenched. In hot weather, black absorbed instead of reflected the sun's rays. She had thought only of putting together an outfit, not of how it would feel. She hoped the khaki shirt wasn't damp. That would show.

Heat radiated up from the concrete walk. A magnolia tree spread its branches over the lawn, but none of the shade reached her.

She pressed the doorbell. What if they weren't home? There was a car in the driveway, half under the magnolia.

Inside the house a child's voice called and seemed to be cut off in midshout. Lily felt a jolt of excitement.

She was about to ring again when she heard footsteps. The door was opened by a freckled young woman with sandy hair and no makeup. She wore pink shorts and a halter top, and carried a dish towel.

"I'm sorry to bother you," Lily said. "I'm looking for this address." She showed a piece of paper on which the writing was deliberately illegible. "It looks like thirty-nine, but I don't find any thirty-nine. I wonder if it might be thirty-seven. Do you know a John Camden?''

The woman pushed back a damp lock of hair. ''No, I don't. If you don't mind—''

Lily eased herself into the doorway. ''I don't know what to do. I've got to find him. Would it be all right if I use your phone? I'll only be a minute. It's a local call.''

The face became stony. ''I'm not supposed to let people in. My husband says it isn't safe.''

''Oh, I understand. It's the same in Chicago. That's where I'm from. I just got in this morning. Believe me, I don't mean any harm. I only want to call and check the address. I haven't any change for a pay phone.''

She shouldn't have said that. The woman might offer her some. Or suggest making the call for her. She had to get into the house.

''Is your husband home? Could I ask him?''

''He's not here.''

This might be the only chance they would have. Lily tried to calm herself.

''Look, why don't you hold my bag, if it makes you feel better. You know, like security.'' She offered her purse. ''I have to tell you, I wouldn't be too thrilled either about letting a stranger into my house. I can understand perfectly.''

Her desperate ideas were almost laughable, but she

must have done something right. With a small, grudging smile, the woman took her purse.

"Maybe it's all right for a minute." She was young, perhaps twenty-one or -two, and seemed a nice person. Undoubtedly she was only obeying orders, helping out her husband's friend. They had probably sold her a bill of goods about Susan and the custody situation.

When they reached the living room, the girl hesitated. Lily could see down a hallway. The master bedroom might have been there and perhaps a telephone, but it was too far into the house. A closer phone was in the kitchen, where the girl reluctantly led her.

The reason for her hesitation became clear. There was a baby in a high chair, a younger one in a plastic infant seat, and a little boy playing with crayons at the table. Lily recognized the Harding children. Her pulse speeded up, making her dizzy. She found the wall phone and lifted its receiver.

Then she put it back. "Could you give me the address book out of my bag? It's a little green one."

All this was such a waste of time that she could scarcely keep from shaking. But her act had to be followed through. There must be no suspicion.

After digging for a while, the woman found her book. Lily managed a bland smile as her eyes traveled over the children, all of whom watched her. She refrained from any comment.

Taking the book, she tried deep breathing. Tried to relax her tense face.

It was a gray telephone in a pink-and-gray kitchen. She dialed the number they had entered that morning for the fictitious Mr. Camden. It reached a cellular phone in the police van outside.

"Hello, is this . . . " She almost asked for George. "Is this John Camden? This is Liz, from Chicago. Yes, I'm here, but I can't find your house. Number thirty-nine Pequot Street? Oh, *Kumquat?* Silly me!" She slapped the side of her head and pretended to listen to directions. Then it was over. They had agreed not to give a code by phone about the children's presence. Probably they thought she would screw it up.

"Thank you *so* much," she told the woman. "It was all a mistake. I can't read his writing. Guess he should have been a doctor, right?"

Another feeble smile. A tremulous one. Lily glanced again at the children. With two so close in age, she might well have asked, "Are they all yours?" She didn't dare. But it would have been pointed to ignore them.

"What sweet kids," she said with the disinterest of one who has no children and couldn't care less. "They must keep you busy."

"That's for sure," said the girl as she conducted her back to the door. They both almost forgot Lily's purse.

"I can't thank you enough," Lily said, taking it from her. "Have a real nice day."

And a nice life, even though George and your husband will probably kill you.

She got into the car. The woman still watched from the doorway. Lily pretended to straighten her hair in the rearview mirror, and wished the shaking would stop.

She waved to the woman, who finally left. Now for the window button, the nearest one on the top row. She had that memorized.

Nothing happened.

The engine, darn it. She turned it on and pressed the button again. Her nervous hand hit the wrong one. A back window went down. Quickly she raised it and tried again.

Hot, humid air poured in, in spite of the air conditioning. Across the street the men puttered convincingly, measuring and making chalk marks.

Come on, guys! What was she supposed to do, just sit there?

She put the car in gear, which took some concentration because the indicator was not on the steering column, where she expected it, but on the dashboard.

When she looked up again there were no men and no orange pylons. The van moved slowly to the end of the block, made a U-turn at the intersection, and came back, parking several yards behind her. She saw them get out and creep toward the house. Two went around to the back. Al got out and stood on the sidewalk with a clipboard, making notes. He wore a hard hat, looking very convincing—and rather sexy.

She tried to be convincing too, edging her car forward. She stopped when two policemen pounded on the door of the house.

Everything stopped. Even her thumping heart.

It seemed forever. The waiting.

One of the officers called, "It's the police, ma'am. Open up!"

Lily crouched low, barely peering over the edge of the window. This was her first dirty trick. She supposed it was necessary under the circumstances, but she felt ashamed.

Maybe they would go easy on the girl. Still, what a shock to find herself surrounded by police. But she must have known it could happen. She must have known the children were there illegally, since they were never allowed outside.

Finally the door opened. From her low angle it was hard to see what was happening, and the magnolia tree blocked part of her view.

She saw people milling about on the stoop. Saw the young woman come out with her hands on her head, like a criminal.

I made this happen, Lily thought, feeling hollow.

Something flashed at the side of her vision. It was Al's arm, beckoning her.

She cringed. She did not want the woman to see her. But her boss was calling.

Suddenly her mind flashed back to the scene at the office with Susan weeping for her children and describing her husband's abuse.

Lily got out of the car. Al beckoned impatiently. She couldn't look at the young, frightened girl who was led past her to a police car.

"My baby!" cried the girl. "I can't leave my baby!"

A policewoman dashed up the steps.

"Go with her." Al gave Lily a push. "Get the Harding kids."

Lily hurried after the officer. She hadn't thought anyone else was in the house, but what if the men were there, and armed?

The policewoman stood waiting for her. She was black and pretty. Lily showed her to the kitchen. The baby in the plastic infant seat was alone, sucking on a pacifier.

"They're not here! They were here just a minute ago."

More than a minute. It had taken awhile for the woman to open her door.

"She must have hidden them. She couldn't have passed them out to anyone, could she?"

"I don't see how," said the officer. "We have the place surrounded." She wiped a drool from the baby's chin.

Maybe there was someone else in the house. The police had already begun a search of the rooms. Lily started down the hall to the master bedroom.

The officer held her back. "Better let me do it. You're a civilian."

Lily caught her breath. What if the children weren't found? No one would believe they had been there.

A warm body came up next to her and took her arm. It was Al. "No kids?"

"They were here. She must have hidden them. They were right here at this table." Even the crayons had been swept away.

"You recognized them? The Harding kids?"

"Yes, Al, I did. I'm not stupid."

"I have great respect for your intelligence, Miss Penn State. But sometimes people get excited and see what they want or expect to see."

"It *was* the Harding children. There were three kids in here. And just now you heard her calling for her baby, not her kids. So the other two weren't hers."

"Let's hope. Anyway, you did okay."

Not if the children were lost again. She felt sick.

Voices came from down the hall. A child's cry. She started toward it.

Al stopped her. "Let the cops do this. We're unofficial, remember."

"They'll be scared."

"Yes, it would have been better if the lady of the house brought them out, but she wasn't cooperating."

The policewoman came first, carrying the little girl.

"They were locked in a walk-in closet," she said. "I don't know how that woman expected they wouldn't make noise."

The boy was crying. Stacey Harding only stared with huge gray eyes as the officer handed her to Lily.

"You're going home to Mommy," Lily said in a loud voice, hoping to cheer the boy.

"Mommy doesn't want us," he sniffled. "Daddy said so."

"Yes, she does. She wants you very much. She was crying for you."

They went outside with all three children. Lily asked, "What about their paterfamilias?" forgetting that Al might not understand.

He did. "He's not our problem. They'll pick him up. We were hired to get the kids."

They drove to the police station. Lily waited on a bench with the children.

After a long time, Al appeared and drew her aside.

"We can't take them with us. Obviously they match the pictures, but without the father, there's no legally positive ID. I've called Mrs. Harding. She'll be coming here early in the morning. She can't get a flight today."

"So that's why I needed a nightgown," Lily said.

His eyes lit up briefly. "We're not obligated to stay, since they won't leave the kids in our custody. But we will anyway, to coordinate things."

"What are they doing with the children?" she asked in alarm.

"They'll be taken care of. Child Welfare, or whatever they call it here."

"But that's so frightening! All these people are

strangers. They won't understand. And none of this is their fault.''

"It's one of the things people don't think about when they start playing football with kids. Not that anybody expects to get caught.''

"I don't think George cared much how they felt. He told them their mother didn't want them.''

"That happens a lot in cases like this. Or telling them the other parent is dead. When people snatch kids, usually it's not done in the best interests of the child. Shall we go?''

She kissed the children good-bye. Kevin clung to her and had to be peeled away by a social worker.

"You'll be okay, honey,'' Lily promised. "Mommy's coming tomorrow. These people will take care of you tonight, and then you'll go home with Mommy.''

She turned to Al. "This is so cruel.''

"I know. It can't be helped. Don't let it get to you.''

"But couldn't we—''

"I explained why not, okay? You can't get emotionally involved, Lily. It's a rule of the game. Come on, I'll take you to dinner.''

Chapter Twelve

Lily collapsed onto an armchair in her motel room. "That was a searing experience."

"A what?" asked Al.

"Horrible. Those poor kids. That poor girl at the house. Maybe you're used to this kind of thing, but I'm not."

He sat down on the edge of the bed. "It doesn't get easier. It's always tough, but somebody's got to do it."

"I wonder what's going to happen to her. I thought she was so innocent, but obviously she knew to hide the kids."

"Don't worry about it, Lily. You have to learn to

separate yourself. It's the same when you're practicing law.''

''I know.'' But knowing didn't help much.

''You ready for dinner?''

They found a restaurant called Uncle Jim's, and ordered fried chicken. ''Might as well try the southern cuisine,'' Al said.

''How do you get used to things like that?'' Lily asked, sipping her water.

Al buttered a hot roll. ''You get used to it because you have to. Anyway, it could have been worse. Nobody got hurt—physically.''

''Emotional hurt can be just as bad.''

''Don't forget,'' he reminded her, ''it was their father, not us, that got them into that. So stop feeling bad. Put the blame where it belongs.'' He pushed the bread basket toward her.

''You're right. He would have given them plenty of emotional hurt. He already did, according to Susan. And this proves he was capable of it.''

''So let's move on. I'm sorry about your weekend.''

''That's okay. It was really interesting. If I were home, I'd be doing the laundry and . . . Oh, no. I forgot to tell Donald I can't see him tomorrow.''

''Do you want to call him?''

''I will later. He's going to be mad.'' She found that oddly undisturbing.

''Doesn't like to have his plans disrupted?''

''He doesn't like anything disrupted. He's quite

stuffy, actually. These are good. Sort of like baking powder biscuits.''

"I can't see you with a stuffy guy, Minnesota."

"I am *not* from Minnesota." She tried to think of something more to say, some answer to his comment, but she couldn't.

"He wasn't always stuffy," she finally replied. "I guess life with him will be very predictable." She went on musing. "Always the same vacation spot. The same dinner on Sunday. Every Christmas and birthday a black lace nightgown, because that's what he'll think he's supposed to do."

"Black lace, huh?" Al seemed immoderately interested.

"If you had a wife, what would you give her?"

"That would depend on who she is."

"Now, you see? That's not Donald. He'd just think in terms of what would be expected in a given situation. Nothing about who *I* am. I happen to like black lace, but I'd want it to be for that reason, not just because it's appropriate."

"You like black lace?"

"I kind of wish I hadn't brought it up. Al, don't you have even one girlfriend?"

He stared past her. His scar was white again. "Not at the moment."

"Where did that scar come from?"

"This?" He touched it. "I cut myself shaving."

"That's not a shaving cut."

"Okay, okay, Minnesota. You know, I like that for a name."

"Just don't call me Minnie for short."

He didn't seem to hear her. "Since you have to know my personal history, I'll tell you. I got this scar in an auto accident. It was just after high school. My girl-friend was driving. She'd had a couple of drinks."

"How old was she?" Lily asked. "You can't drink until you're twenty-one in New York State."

"Did I say it was legal? I said she had a couple. Maybe more. We both did. She was a beautiful girl, Denise. She had long hair, a little darker than yours, and brown eyes."

"I hardly dare ask, but what happened?"

"She couldn't make it around a corner. Crashed into an overpass. That was out on the Island."

"Was she hurt?"

"She was DOA. I walked away with this scar."

And a lot of bitterness, Lily thought. "That's why you don't drink?"

"Would you? It's disgusting."

She was glad she hadn't touched liquor in his presence.

"But you must have had girlfriends since then."

"A few. Nothing serious."

"You really loved her."

"I did, but there's no happy memories. It didn't have to happen. I'm angry at both of us for drinking, and at me for not driving and for getting out alive."

"That's quite a lot to carry around," Lily said.

"I manage."

"But if you haven't had a serious relationship since then, maybe it left you with a problem."

A wry smile touched his mouth. "What were you, a psych major?"

"Actually, yes. It was more interesting than biology or chem."

"Put it this way. Maybe I just haven't found the right person."

"That could have something to do with it," she agreed. "But it doesn't have to be your ideal. I mean, who's perfect?"

Her salad arrived, smothered in creamy dressing. "I think I like southern food. How come all these people aren't fat?"

"I thought your medical student was supposed to be ideal," Al said.

"On the surface, maybe, but everybody has some faults. I really thought you and Rochelle were seeing each other."

"Yeah, you told me. How come?"

"It was my first day. She said, and I quote, 'I know he's attractive, but don't get your hopes up.' "

"She said that, huh?" He seemed tickled.

"I don't know where she got the idea that I'd be thinking along those lines. I told her I was engaged."

"Good going." He had a pleased grin that slowly broadened. "With all due modesty, she did make a play for me, but I thought she moved on. Found greener pastures, and all that.''

''Maybe she was just warning me that you wouldn't be receptive if I tried. Not that I had any intention of it.''

''Of course not, when you have a stuffy medical student,'' he agreed.

Later, in her motel room, she lay awake thinking of Al asleep in his bed just the other side of the wall. It was odd, but she had never pictured Donald asleep in bed. She and Donald had drifted together quite naturally. Their relationship worked. It was meant to be. And it had never felt like this.

I'll get over it, she told herself. *It's just because I've had an exciting day.*

She reviewed it from the beginning: their ride to the airport, holding his hand on the plane, Al in the hard hat, taking notes. She kept going back to Al, almost forgetting the children.

I'll get over it, she decided again, and forced her mind to drift.

At eleven in the morning, they went to pick up Susan Harding. She looked paler than ever, and more worn.

''I won't get my hopes up until I see them,'' she said. ''Until I have them.''

''Believe me, they're okay,'' said Al. It was the first time he and Susan had met face to face. ''Maybe not too happy at the moment, but as soon as they see you and get back home, they'll be fine.''

''What about George?''

''He hasn't shown up yet. Don't worry. The police will be watching for him.''

'' 'Don't worry' is easier said than done,'' Susan replied. ''But at least I'll have my kids.''

An hour later, she had them. Four hours after that, they were all on a plane heading back to New York. After dropping off the Hardings at their apartment, Al drove Lily home.

''It's been a really fun weekend,'' she told him when they reached her building.

''I hope you mean that. Maybe we could do it again sometime.'' He grinned.

''Whenever you say.''

She went upstairs to an empty apartment. That was a letdown. She had looked forward to giving Pat and Charlene a full account of her adventure. But it was a beautiful afternoon. There was no reason why they should stay home.

In the kitchen she found a note signed by Charlene. *We took Donald out because he was lonely. Hope you don't mind.*

Oh, really. That was interesting. She made herself a baloney sandwich, then watched the news and *60 Minutes*, followed by *Murder, She Wrote*. It was a rerun, but she hadn't remembered the end and didn't mind seeing it again.

When it was over, she stretched out on her bed and gazed at the ceiling. Her head filled with memories of Greensboro—and Al. . . .

She woke to the sound of Charlene tiptoeing around the room.

"I was trying to be quiet!" Charlene protested. "How did it go?"

"We got them," Lily said. "It was the weirdest thing I've ever done. And exciting. The police were there, pretending to be road workers. They sent me into the house first to see if the kids were there. I was an undercover agent, Charlene! For maybe seven minutes I was an undercover agent."

"Wasn't that dangerous?"

"No, the only ones there were a girl, maybe younger than I am, and three kids. I felt bad when they took her away, but she stuffed those kids in a closet so we wouldn't find them, and she must have terrorized them into keeping quiet. So after that I didn't feel so bad. Where did you go today?"

"First we took the Circle Line cruise all around Manhattan. Then we went to Chinatown for dinner, and then a movie."

"The two of you and Donald?"

"That's right. I hope you don't mind."

"Not at all. Thanks for looking after him." Lily closed her eyes and went back to sleep.

Reporting to the office on Monday seemed strangely anticlimactic after that weekend.

Al was there ahead of her. "What time do you usually get here in the morning?" Lily asked.

"Around seven-thirty, eight," he said. "You are not required to beat me to it."

A few minutes later, José rang the doorbell.

"The police, they come and ask more questions," he complained, with an angry look at Lily. "I don't hurt no old lady."

"I'm sure you didn't," said Al. "Just hang in there till somebody tries to fence that bracelet."

"What if they don't plan to fence it?" Lily asked. "Maybe they only took it to look like a robbery."

Al's eyebrows rose a fraction of an inch. "Who did you have in mind?"

"Her husband was planning a new TV project and he might lose his backing if there were a scandal. If those pictures got out."

"The pictures weren't scandalous," said Al. "They just showed him with a woman. In one of them he had his hand on her butt. They didn't get any racier than that."

"Yes, but if she wasn't his wife, and this was a children's series with sponsors of children's products—"

"She definitely wasn't his wife. Poles apart." Al chuckled.

José didn't share his amusement. "What am I supposed to do? They are trying to break me down or something?''

"I doubt it," said Al. "They're stumped, that's all. Poor guy.''

"Do you mean Mr. Rodriguez?" Lily asked. "Or Muldoon?''

"I meant Muldoon. It'll work out, José. Don't worry about it.''

"I don't want no more questions," said the worried super.

"Can't blame you for that. Lily, call the jewelry company and set up an appointment. I'll go over there so I can look at the place. And"—he handed her a crumpled paper from his pocket—"make this into a nice bill for Susan Harding.''

José remained where he was, glaring at Lily and flexing his hands as though he might like to strangle her. He had on his usual work clothes, a dark green shirt and pants, with an enormous pair of yellow gloves protruding from the rear pocket.

"Maybe I go home to Mayagüez," he told her darkly. "But there I can't find no work.''

"I'm sure Al's right," she said. "If they don't come up with any evidence, they'll get off your back and start looking somewhere else.''

"What they gonna find?" The hands flexed again. "Why don't this big-shot detective Barberini go figure out what happened?''

"It's a police matter, Mr. Rodriguez. He's not supposed to interfere. Is there something wrong with your hands?''

He stopped flexing and looked at them. ''Nothin' wrong.''

''Do you have arthritis? It must be hard to work with your hands if they hurt.''

He shot her another hostile look, turned abruptly, and left.

She stared after him, wondering at that indignation. Was it all a pretense? Even the sad eyes? Maybe the police knew what they were doing.

She called the jewelry company. She typed the bill for Susan Harding and put it in the mail. Then she read the Lanken file again.

She called AFTRA and learned that Sharon May was a member. They wouldn't give her Sharon's address.

''Listen,'' Lily said. ''My boss is considering Miss May for a role in a new series. How do I get hold of her?''

''Miss May is in a series right now,'' they replied. ''Who's your boss?''

''Donald Flynn. He's a producer.''

''Maybe you could reach her through Aries Talent. They're on Broadway and Fifty-first.''

With no idea how to approach this, she punched in the number for Aries Talent. ''Yes. This is Donald Flynn's office calling. I wonder if you can give me some information on Sharon May. I'd like to know

about her background, what work she's done, and how
I can reach her.''

"You can reach her through us,'' the agency said.
"Sure, I can give you a publicity kit. Where should I
send it?''

"I'd like it right now. How about if I send someone
to pick it up?'' Lily offered.

She took an early lunch hour. Al didn't mind, as
long as she was back by one-thirty. She hurried to the
subway, then waited ten frustrating minutes for a train.

The home of Aries Talent was a seedy building in
the middle of the block. At least it had an elevator,
which she shared with a leering, tobacco-chewing mes-
senger. When he edged closer to her as the car crept
upward, she said, "You know, that stuff can give you
cancer of the mouth.''

The elevator bumped to a stop, depositing her in
Aries's reception room. It was as crowded as Macy's
on a Saturday. Most of the people, she deduced, were
actors looking for work. She was bounced to several
people before finding the one she had talked to, who
handed her a manila envelope.

"We'll be in touch,'' Lily said, and left quickly.
She wanted to ask questions, but was more afraid of
being questioned herself.

As she walked back to the subway, opening her
envelope for a peek at the hot pink folder inside, someone grabbed her arm.

"He-e-ey!" said a silvery voice. "What's a nice girl like you doing in these parts?"

"Oh . . . hello, Rochelle. I was just running an errand for my roommate. She works in the Bronx and can't get down here."

Rochelle stood beaming, with the sun shining on her hair. She really was a friendly person. Lily asked, "How did your audition go?"

"Who knows? They either call you back or they don't. You wanna have lunch?"

"I really have to get back to the office. Al has a two-o'clock appointment."

"It's not even one. How about coffee?"

Rochelle was a co–worker, and also involved in the Lanken case. Lily followed her into a coffee shop where they managed to find a booth at the rear.

"What sort of errand are you doing for your roommate?" Rochelle asked.

"Just picking up some material she wanted. Tell me something. Are you the one who took those famous Lanken pictures? It says R.P."

"Yeah, that was me. Why?"

"I just wondered. This whole field is so interesting. How do you do it? Do you burst into people's motel rooms?"

"Oh, no. That's old stuff, when the only grounds for divorce in New York State was adultery. Now you don't have to catch them in fragrant . . . whatever it is."

"In flagrante delicto," Lily supplied.

"What are you, a lawyer?"

"No. I would like to be, someday. What do you do, just catch them together? And how do you do it without being seen?"

"Telephoto lens. I usually wear a scarf so they can't see my hair."

"Yes, your hair is rather memorable."

"Oh, it's nothing. In show business everybody does things with their hair. There's a lot of platinum blondes. I just wish I could get a new mouth. I know mine's kind of big. But so is Loni Anderson's, you know? And it doesn't hurt her any. It's all in how you fix yourself up."

"That's true." Lily caught a whiff of lemon yogurt. She remembered the evening Donald had brought some over. This was what it reminded her of.

"What's that scent you have on?" she asked. "It's different."

"It's called Limón. That's Spanish for lemon."

"Yes, that's what it smells like. Do you speak Spanish?" Lily asked.

"Oh no, not me. Just a little, maybe. From high school."

"You could practice on José."

Rochelle gave a laugh like broken glass. "Yeah. Sometimes."

"How's Mrs. Lanken doing? Have you heard anything?"

"I don't know. I don't ask."

"I wonder what sort of person *he* is, married to someone like her."

"How would I know? The only time I saw him was through a telephoto lens."

"I was just curious. What does Sharon May look like?"

"Who's that?" Rochelle spread her fingers, examining the nails.

"His girlfriend. The one you took pictures of."

"Oh, her. She's tall. Red hair. Her mouth is smaller than mine."

Most people's were. Lily took a five-dollar bill from her wallet. "I really have to get back."

Rochelle's hand came down on hers. "Oh, no. This is on me."

"No, please. Why should you?"

"Put that away. It was my idea, doing this."

"Well, okay." Lily put away the bill. "Next time it's my treat."

"I'll remember that!" Rochelle chuckled. The broad smile followed Lily out to the sidewalk and into the subway station.

Chapter Thirteen

Men wear perfume too, she reminded herself.

The brown envelope was there on her desk, but she did not dare study its contents until Al had left. At one-thirty he came out of his office, pulling on a dark blue suit jacket.

"By the way," said Lily, "how's Mrs. Lanken?"

"She's mending. Why?"

"Just thought I'd ask. Do you remember telling me that when people suffer a trauma like that, they forget whatever happened just before as well as after it?"

"Head trauma, usually." He took a comb from his breast pocket and applied it to his hair.

"Then how can Mrs. Lanken remember smelling perfume at the time she was attacked?"

153

"I wouldn't know. Everybody's different. Maybe it's a false memory."

"There's another thing. You said whoever did it meant to kill her."

"It's what I'm assuming, although in this business assumptions can be dangerous. I wasn't stating a fact, Lily."

"I realize that. I just wondered how come they failed, unless they didn't have the strength to pull it really tight. A person with weak hands, for instance."

"That's an assumption I'm not going to make."

"Wait, Al." She got up from her desk, took the comb from his hand, and arranged his hair more neatly.

"Thanks," he said. "That's a service even Mrs. Crocker never gave me."

"Glad to be of assistance." She drew in a breath, but this was not the time to ask him about the job. Not when he was hurrying off.

Taking the hot pink folder out of its envelope, she read about Sharon May. The pictures showed a blue-eyed redhead with a lithe figure in various poses and varying degrees of dress. She was twenty-six years old, born in Clifton, New Jersey.

"New Jersey!" That could provide an opening wedge.

Sharon was currently appearing in a series called *Hopes and Dreams,* which was located in a studio on East Fourteenth Street.

Perfect!

The telephone rang. "Barberini," Lily answered, enjoying the sound of the syllables.

"I was so upset about Bobby," Mary Whelan began in a watery voice, "I forgot to ask how much I owe you."

Lily gulped. Not being a licensed investigator herself, she was not allowed to take money, and Al had wanted no part of the case.

"I, uh . . . I don't have the bill ready yet, Miss Whelan. I'll send it to you, okay?"

She simply wouldn't send one, that was all. Whelan couldn't complain about that.

Another call to Aries Talent got her a phone number for the studio where *Hopes and Dreams* was made. The studio told her the day's taping was still going on.

"When do you expect it to finish?" Lily asked.

"Usually about five or six o'clock."

That was vague, but she would try it anyway. She called Elissa Brock.

"I need some more information on Mr. Dembrovsky," Lily said.

"You're really going to do this for me?"

"I'm going to try, and I'm doing it without my boss, so if you call, be sure to ask for me."

"I will. And don't forget, James knew me as Elissa Mahon."

James Dembrovsky was an artist, Elissa said.

"A real artist?"

"Maybe you could call him an artisan. He was always making things with his hands. Little sculptures. Things like that.''

''Where was he living at the time you knew him?'' Lily asked.

''He was on Greenwich Street. But the building isn't there anymore. I went and looked.''

''Do you think he might have become an artist professionally?''

''I have no idea. It's hard to earn a living that way.''

''You say you hired someone who traced a James Dembrovsky that turned out to be deceased. Could that possibly be a relative? His father, maybe? Was your James a Junior?''

''I don't know that.'' Elissa's voice faded. James Dembrovsky seemed to go with it, as though he were more an ideal than a real person. Like Bobby Decatur.

''You don't know his father's name?''

''No, I don't.'' A whisper.

''Do you know when and where this James Dembrovsky died?''

''About three years ago. It was a nursing home in the Bronx. The Sunrise Manor.''

''Sunrise. That's better than Sunset, I guess, for a nursing home.'' Lily reached for the Bronx directory.

''The detective traced him from that Greenwich Street address,'' Elissa said sadly. ''After that it was Charles Street, and then I don't know.'' She began to cry.

Lily called the Sunrise Manor. ''This is the Greenwich Village Bureau of Records. We understand you had a patient there named James Dembrovsky, who died about three years ago. Can you give me the date of his death?''

''Greenwich Village Bureau of Records?'' they asked doubtfully.

''We're a quasi-official organization. We keep track of Greenwich Village residents for reasons I don't need to go into at this time. Can you give me some information on James Dembrovsky?''

''Just a minute. I'll have to check.''

Lily hoped she was checking a computer and not a supervisor who would call her bluff.

Seconds went by. Maybe minutes. Then the voice returned.

''James Dembrovsky died almost three years ago on July seventeenth. He was eighty-two years old. The last known address was Horatio Street in Manhattan.''

''Thank you. I appreciate this,'' Lily said. ''Do you know if he had any relatives?''

''He had a daughter, Elizabeth Winston, who looked after his affairs. She was on West Twenty-third Street.''

''West Twenty-third. I'm really grateful. Excuse me, I have another call. Thanks for your help.''

It was a job applicant, who inquired dolefully, ''I don't suppose it's still open. I saw it in last week's paper.''

''It's not running today?'' Lily asked.

"No, and it wasn't in the Sunday paper. So I don't suppose it's still open."

"I haven't heard anything about that. You could send in your résumé." Lily gave the address.

What did it mean? Had he found someone? Why didn't he tell her?

She tried searching his desk, careful not to disturb anything, but gave up quickly. What if he dusted the place for fingerprints?

She looked around his office, not having seen much of it before. His computer was still turned on, with a Star Trek screensaver. It made her smile.

A massive cabinet stood in a corner of the room. It was a great old-fashioned wardrobe made of solid oak. Listening for any sound from the front door, she opened it.

She had expected papers or other office material, but it was full of clothes, men's and women's clothing of all kinds: dress clothes, sports clothes, even a tuxedo. She found the blue dress and the white blazer Rochelle had been wearing when she left the office last Wednesday afternoon.

So it wasn't something she had brought with her to change into at her home away from home. She had chosen it from this collection, which was probably kept on hand for disguise and surveillance purposes.

Had she been leaving to go on a job? Most likely. She had walked out purposefully.

Lily remembered what she herself had been wearing

that day—her blue chambray skirt and white blouse. This dress was almost the same shade of blue.

She took another call. It was the Greensboro police. They had apprehended George Harding.

"We just thought you'd like to know," they said.

When Al came in a few minutes later, she gave him the message.

"Call the wife," he told her. "She can rest easier knowing he's in custody."

After Lily had delivered that information, she looked up Winston in the Manhattan directory.

"This is ridiculous," she said aloud. "Why am I looking up Winston? Why not Dembrovsky?"

There were fewer Dembrovskys than Winstons, but no James Dembrovsky. She reviewed Chapter One of *How to Find Out Anything about Anybody*.

The phone book—that was what it said. Always go to the phone book first. It didn't invariably work, but according to her manual it was successful more often than most people expected.

She tried the Bronx, where the nursing home was. She was looking up Brooklyn and Queens when a chorus of barks erupted outside the window.

The five Pekingese dogs were being pulled across the sidewalk by their agitated mistress to make way for a friendly German shepherd, probably a young one, with tail wagging, wanting to make friends.

The dogs walked on. *They were there*, thought Lily,

and ran out to the street. The Pekingese group had disappeared.

She went to examine the iron gate through which José took out the garbage. It covered the entrance to a narrow passageway between buildings. No one could have gotten over or around it. She grasped one of its bars and rattled it. The lock was tight.

She went back inside to find Al waiting by her desk. "Where did you go?"

"I went out to try to catch a possible witness," she said.

"Witness to what?"

"There's a woman who walks five Pekingese dogs—"

"Yeah, I've seen her."

"They were passing this building right around the time Mrs. Lanken was attacked. I just wondered if she might have seen somebody go in."

"How could she see anybody if you didn't? They'd have to pass your line of vision to get in."

"I was thinking of that gate."

"Lily, nobody has a key for that except José."

"He has arthritic hands," she said. "He didn't want to talk about it."

"Maybe he's afraid he'll lose his job if they think he's disabled."

"He might also have trouble pulling something tight around someone's neck."

"I admire your creativity, Minnesota, but why don't

you leave this up to the police? They won't want you poking around. You could muddy up their investigation. And let me point out that the police not only have to find the perpetrator, they also have to gather enough evidence to make a case that will stand up in a court of law. If you screw that up, they won't be happy.''

''I understand. But what I don't like is the police suspecting *me*.''

''You said they suspect me too,'' he reminded her. ''It's not fun, but it will blow over. How about typing up this agreement with the jewelry company, and then this report on our weekend adventure?''

Chastened, she went back to her secretarial duties. The IBM typewriter was a correcting Selectric, exactly what she had used at the magazine.

She finished the agreement and took it in to Al. He was on the phone and nodded an acknowledgment. While he was occupied, she took the opportunity to make a quick search through the Staten Island directory.

She tried Nassau County. Westchester County.

Dembrovsky, James. Croton-on-Hudson.

He wouldn't be home. He probably commuted to a job in the city. He would not be home until maybe seven o'clock. She could call him from her apartment.

As though it had a life of its own, her hand reached toward the phone. Al was on another line. She could see the lit button.

She punched in the numbers. One, then the area

code, nine one four. His number. It began to ring. Three times. If anyone answered, it would be a woman or a child.

It was a man. Lily found she was nearly out of breath. She felt birds flying around in her chest.

"Is this . . . Mr. Dembrovsky?"

"Yes." It was spoken with a pleasant, expectant lilt.

"Mr. James Dembrovsky who used to live in Greenwich Village?"

"That's right." His interest was piqued, she could tell.

"Did you know someone named Elissa Mahon?"

There was a pause. A catching of breath. "Elissa." He savored it, a name he hadn't spoken in many years.

"This is a private detective agency, Mr. Dembrovsky. Elissa Mahon hired us to see if we could find you."

"Where is Elissa?" The words tumbled out.

"She's here in New York City. She told me that when she was a girl, her parents took her to California and wouldn't let her have any contact with you. She's been married, widowed, and has two grown children. Now she's hoping to see you again, or at least talk to you, if you're at all interested."

"Yes, *yes!* Tell me . . . tell me . . . "

"I'll give you her number. Do you have a pencil?"

Al came out of his office. Lily looked him straight

in the eye and gave James Dembrovsky Elissa's number. "Good luck, Mr. Dembrovsky."

"What was that?" asked Al.

"I'm sorry. I shouldn't be making personal calls at the office."

"It wasn't personal, was it? Are you finding more lost lovers? Don't you ever give up? Lily, take this down to the jewelry company and bring it back signed. They're on Lafayette Street. Do you know where that is?"

"It goes into Canal," she said.

"Yes, they're down at the Canal Street end. Take your time. I'll be here."

She took a subway, never minding the hot bodies and the smell of soot. She was far away from them. Through her efforts, two people had fulfilled a lifelong wish—she hoped. If they didn't like each other after they met again, that was not her responsibility.

The president of the jewelry company was a chunky man named Jacoby. He wore suspenders and a yarmulke, and insisted on whispering and trying to keep Lily out of sight.

"We can't let them *know*," he explained, pushing her into a corner. "We don't know who it is yet." He read the entire agreement and finally signed it.

"I'm sure you'll be very happy with Mr. Barberini's work." She left a copy with him and went back to the subway.

Thank goodness it was almost rush hour. The trains

ran more frequently now, although they were crowded. She reached Fourteenth Street and walked rapidly eastward. Al would be expecting her back with his copy of the contract. Or maybe he would think she had gone straight home.

She reached the studio where *Hopes and Dreams* was taped. It had more than one entrance. She found an obscure one at the side and hoped that was the stage door. If it wasn't, she was out of luck.

Twenty minutes went by with no one coming or going. She would be picked up for loitering. Possibly, if the police put it all together, for stalking Sharon May.

The door flew open. A man came out, young and good-looking, with lively blue eyes. She had never seen the series, but thought he must be an actor, with all that personality and presence.

"Excuse me," Lily said. "Do you know if Sharon May is in there?"

"Yes, she is." He smiled. "Are you a fan?"

"Well, I haven't exactly seen the show. I was sent by a New Jersey magazine to interview her. She comes from New Jersey, doesn't she?"

"I couldn't tell you. Why don't you go on in?" He held the door open.

"Thank you." She darted through it and up a flight of steps.

She was in a corridor. She could hear voices. Thumping and bumping, and scraping. She stopped a man in overalls and asked for Sharon May. He pointed to a closed door. It was the women's dressing room. A cacophony of voices drowned out her knock. She opened the door.

In a moment of trepidation, she wished she could have taped and watched at least one episode of the show. But she hadn't even known about it until today. Everything was happening too fast.

She recognized Sharon May sitting by herself at the end of a long, mirrored dressing table. She had removed her screen makeup and her face had a sad, puffy look.

Lily walked over to her. "Miss May?"

Sharon looked up and saw her in the mirror, then turned.

"I'm Lily Foster, doing an article for *Suburban Nights,* on New Jersey natives in the entertainment industry. Do you have a minute or two?"

The actress took a moment to think about it, then answered resignedly, "I guess. What do you want to know?"

"I read your press kit." Which, darn it, she had left on her desk. "So I know about your career. What we're more interested in is the personal angle. Does your family still live in New Jersey?"

"No. Florida."

"I see. Do you have any, well, romantic interests? I understand you've been seeing the TV producer, Barry Lanken."

Sharon's face flared. "How did you know about that?"

Lily had taken it too fast and plunged into quicksand.

"Those things get around, I'm afraid. If it's supposed to be secret, I won't mention it."

Turning back to the mirror, Sharon took a look at her face and shuddered. "It doesn't matter. It's over."

"Do you mean you're not seeing him anymore?" Lily sat down on an empty chair beside her.

"That's what 'over' means, isn't it?"

"Is that because he's married?"

"No, he was getting divorced so he could marry me. But somebody else moved in. If you print any of this, I'll kill you."

"I won't," Lily promised. "I'm sorry to hear that. Is it serious, this new relationship of his?"

"How would I know? Just some actress trying to further her career. She doesn't care about him."

"Do you know who it is?"

"Some blonde. How would I know?"

"There must be a lot of blond actresses. Is it somebody who works with him? Do you know what she looks like?"

The puffy face turned for a first real look at Lily. "Why do you have to know all this?"

"Well, I'll tell you, we do print a gossip column. But I'll definitely leave you out of it."

A tiny smile spread across Sharon's pale lips. "You won't tell where you got it from?"

"It will be absolutely anonymous."

"I don't know her name, and I doubt that she's been in anything of his. I do know she has silver-blond hair. Out of a bottle, of course. You can tell by her eyes. They're black. Got a king-size mouth. It must take up half her face. She dances too. I think she's been in a couple of Broadway choruses."

"Would you know her name if you heard it?"

"I don't think so. If I try to find out, everybody will think I'm jealous."

"And of course you're not. Miss May, thank you. This is fascinating. I'll come back for your interview when you're feeling more upbeat. By the way, I love you in the show."

Chapter Fourteen

It was five-thirty. Lily approached Al's building from the other side so he wouldn't see her pass the window, if he happened to be watching. She climbed the flight of steps that led to the main entrance and looked for José's doorbell.

It wasn't hard to find. SUPER, it said on a strip of red tape. Apartment 1B.

She rang the bell and waited. He might have been out working at another building. She rang again and heard a click. He called through the intercom, "Yeah, what is it?"

"It's Lily from Mr. Barberini's office."

Again she waited. Finally he buzzed her in. She entered a red-carpeted hallway that smelled of disin-

fectant cleaner. There were two apartments on the
floor. The rear one was open with José lounging in the
doorway. He wore an undershirt and a clean pair of
jeans. His hair was damp and slicked back.

"What do you want?" he demanded, not moving.
From inside came the sound of television.

"I want to ask you . . . I thought no one besides you
had a key for that gate that goes to the back. The one
where you bring out the garbage."

He made no reply except a pensive mumble.

"What does that mean?" she asked. "Someone else
has a key? The landlord, maybe?"

"Nobody else."

"Are you absolutely sure about that?"

He glowered.

"Or," she went on, "did you leave the gate open
by accident?"

"I never leave the gate open. Never."

"Well, then." She narrowed the gap between them
so he couldn't close the door. "You know the police
think you attacked Mrs. Lanken."

"I don't hurt no old ladies."

"I hope you don't. I really do. Did anybody ever
borrow the key, maybe?"

He stood weighing that suggestion for nearly half a
minute. Then he said, "One time I give the key to my
friend, but she gives it back."

"What friend is that?"

"My friend."

"You're not helping yourself, Mr. Rodriguez. Obviously somebody got in there. If it wasn't you, then who was it?"

He clenched his hands. She hadn't meant to confront him so directly.

A middle-aged man entered the building carrying a bag of groceries. He greeted José and started up the stairs. At least there were people around.

"I don't hurt old ladies." José frowned thoughtfully. "Maybe my friend, she gives the key to someone."

"Maybe she had it copied. Who's your friend? Come on."

"You're going to tell the police," he accused her.

"I might not have to. They aren't stupid, you know. Who was it, Rochelle Pulver?"

He drew back and shut the door in her face. She knocked on it.

"Go away," he said.

"There's one more thing. Do you know a woman in this neighborhood who has five little Chinese dogs?"

"What is a Chinese dog?"

"Little fluffy things with flat faces and curly tails. I've seen her walking those dogs and I want to know who she is. My grandmother has a dog like that."

"I don't know who. She live on the corner. Big house."

"Which corner, Mr. Rodriguez?"

He flung the door open and pointed eastward. "That way." Then he shut it again.

She left the building, glancing back at Al's entrance, and walked to the corner. It was a multistory apartment house that faced the avenue. The front door was locked. A wilted-looking man trudged up the sidewalk, carrying a briefcase under his arm, and headed for the entrance.

"Excuse me," Lily said. "Do you live here? Is there a woman in this building who has five Pekingese dogs?"

He inclined his head toward Fifteenth Street. "She's coming now."

Lily went to meet her. The woman had on a pink-and-red muumuu and flip-flop sandals. They made a slapping counterpoint to the pitter-patter of her dogs' feet.

"They're adorable." Lily held out her hand toward a small red one. They crowded around to sniff it. "I've seen you before. I think it's remarkable that you keep them so well groomed."

"They're my babies," said the woman.

"I know you often walk around the block. I saw you Wednesday afternoon with your dogs. I was sitting at my desk on the ground floor. Do you remember Wednesday?"

A shrug. "Like any other day."

"It wasn't for me. A woman visiting my office was attacked and almost killed. I'm in one of the brown-stones in the middle of the block. There's a sign that says 'Barberini.' That's where I work. We have a gate next to the building that goes into a passageway.''

''I know the one you mean.''

''That gate's always locked, but somebody must have opened it and gone through just about the time you were passing by.''

The woman pursed her mouth in thought. She had dull brown eyes and graying hair.

''Sometimes there's a Spanish guy that goes through there,'' she said. ''He brings out the garbage bags and he always has on gloves. Big yellow ones.''

''Yes, but I wondered if there was somebody else.''

''Hey, wait a minute. It was you, remember?''

''Me! Oh, no. I'm talking about—''

''Yeah. I saw you on my earlier walk, over by the corner. You had on a blue dress, I remember that, and you almost got yourself bit by Snappy here.''

''That part is true, but I didn't go in through the gate.''

''It was you, no mistake. I remember you because of Snappy. You came out through the gate, then you saw me and scooted away. A blonde in a blue dress. White top. That was you.''

''I think I understand. Thank you so much. Do you mind giving me your name and address?''

''Oh, no. I don't want to get involved.''

''Well, okay.'' She could always be found later.

The woman dawdled behind with her dogs while Lily went back to the office.

She passed the gate. How easy it would be with a key. Undoubtedly there was one for the back door too, which led into the building from the garden.

When she entered the office, Al was standing by her desk. So was Rochelle Pulver. They were examining something on it, and both turned as Lily came in.

"That took you long enough," said Al.

"I had to wait for the subway," she told him. "Here's your signed agreement."

He took it without looking at it. "Thanks." Then he held up the hot pink folder. Sharon May's press kit. "What's this?"

"Oh . . . that's personal," Lily said.

"Where do you know her from?"

"She's a Jersey girl, like me. I just found that out. I do a little writing for a New Jersey paper sometimes. I was hoping to get an interview. How are you, Rochelle?"

Al said, "You didn't tell me you write for a Jersey paper."

"It's just an occasional thing. There's probably a lot I haven't told you."

He fixed her with his eyes. "Come on, Lily. What's this really for?"

Rochelle stood by, smiling. She was a better actress than Lily.

"What makes you think it's not for what I said?" Lily asked.

"I know you've seen Mrs. Lanken's file."

Finally Rochelle spoke. "That's why you went to Broadway this noon, isn't it? To pick that up. Don't you know it's a police matter?" Her voice was sweet, her smile still in place.

Al added, "You could be hindering the police investigation. I already told you that."

"I don't think so," Lily said. "Anyway, this is old stuff. Sharon May isn't Barry Lanken's bimbo anymore."

Al's face darkened. "What are you talking about?"

Lily took a deep breath and made a decision. If she simply gave the police her facts, they might not believe her. After all, who was she? A nobody. Untrained.

"Sharon May told me," she began, "that somebody else made a move on Barry Lanken and displaced her."

"That's a lie!" Rochelle exclaimed.

"How would you know?" Lily asked. "You took those pictures back in March. Have you been following him ever since?"

"When did you talk to Sharon May?" asked Al.

"I have to admit I stopped off at her studio on the way back here. On my own time. Because I really don't like being suspected of a crime I didn't commit. Neither does José, for that matter, although he did abet it rather innocently."

"What," demanded Al, "are you talking about?" Rochelle was silent.

"José lent a key for that gate to someone," Lily

explained. "He wouldn't say who, but he referred to the person as 'she'. Okay?"

"Uh-huh," said Al. "I'm with you so far."

"He said the person gave it back, so he wasn't suspicious. Apparently it didn't occur to him that she might have had it copied."

Rochelle's smile disappeared.

"There are other pieces of circumstantial evidence," Lily went on.

"Circumstantial," Rochelle said breathily. Then she straightened up. "Al, I have to be going."

"Oh, must you?" Lily pleaded. "This gets interesting."

"I really have to—"

"Stay!" ordered Al. He turned back to Lily. "Make it quick."

"Okay. Sharon May described Barry Lanken's new girlfriend as a silver-blond actress-dancer with dark eyes who's been in a couple of Broadway shows and has a wide mouth."

Rochelle's hand flew to her mouth.

"There's a witness too, sort of," Lily said. "That lady with the five Pekingese dogs was walking by here at about the time of the attack. I found her just now. She says she saw you coming out through the gate."

"*Me?*" screeched Rochelle.

"She described what you had on. Blue and white. You changed to a blue dress and white jacket while you were here. Exactly the same colors I was wearing that day. I doubt if it was a coincidence. You also had on perfume. Mrs. Lanken smelled it when she was attacked. You must have known about her bladder problem. You knew she'd need the bathroom. And there was that nice shower curtain—"

Rochelle's chest heaved. She gasped for breath, hyperventilating. "Al, this is ri*dic*ulous. It's insane. You've known me longer than her. She's just trying to pin it on me. I've got to—"

Al made a dive and seized her arm. "Lily, call the police."

Chapter Fifteen

Pat came out of the kitchen as soon as Lily reached home that night.

"What happened to you? I was worried. It's already eight o'clock. You didn't go for another walk, I hope."

"Oh, no. Nothing like that. A person in our office was arrested, that's all." Lily paced the living room, squeezing her hands together. She was too exhausted to stand up, too wired to sit down. Once the police came, Al had taken over, but he made her stay and tell them what she had told him.

And they listened. That was the most amazing part.

Pat gaped. "Arrested! Not your boss, was it? What did he get arrested for?"

"*Not* my boss. It was one of the investigators. She

179

tried to kill a client. That may sound counterproductive, but the client was making herself inconvenient—''

"Lily!"

"It's okay. It's all over. Where's Charlene?"

"She, uh . . . well, you see, Donald called and you weren't here, and they sort of . . . went out."

"It's okay."

"It is?"

"I think Donald and I are history."

"What are you talking about? You've been going together since college."

"That's true. I thought we wanted the same things out of life, but I've been realizing we don't."

The downstairs buzzer rang. Lily, who was closest, called into the intercom, "Who is it?"

Oscar the doorman's voice came back to her, electronically fuzzy. "Mr. Barberini for Miss Foster."

"Send him up." She turned to Pat. "It's my boss. What am I going to do?"

"About what?"

"Maybe he's sorry we turned her in. Maybe he's coming to fire me."

"He could wait until tomorrow, couldn't he? Bosses don't usually do that in your home."

Lily did not want to share her worst fears. She watched for the elevator, expecting Al to arrive with Muldoon and Washington. Maybe they would question her further, blow holes in her circumstantial evidence—maybe even take her down to the station again.

He was alone. He smiled when he saw her and held up a small rectangular object. "I forgot about this in all the excitement."

It looked like an audiotape. She did not know why he had brought it or what there was to remember about it.

"Pat, this is my boss, Al Barberini. Pat Cotton, my roommate."

He shook Pat's hand. "I thought you had two room-mates."

"The other one's out with my . . . ex-boyfriend."

"Ex-boyfriend, huh? The medical student? You're kidding."

"No," she said, "I'm not. It's been exxing for a while now. I just didn't think about it."

He whistled. "Can't say I'm terribly sorry. But we'll discuss that another time. Does anybody here have a tape recorder?"

Lily and Pat looked at each other. "Mine's broken," said Pat.

"Not even a Walkman? Okay, Minnesota, it looks as if you'll have to come down to my car. Do you mind?"

She hadn't even taken off her shoes yet. She picked up her purse and was ready.

"What's this 'Minnesota'?" Pat asked as they left.

"He forgets my name," said Lily.

Pat winked and gave a thumbs-up sign. She approved of Al.

"What's that thing in your hand?" Lily asked as they rode the elevator down.

"I'll let you hear it first before we talk about it," he said. "I've got a tape deck in my car."

He was double-parked outside her building. "Only place I could find."

"I'm glad you didn't get a ticket."

They settled in his car with the windows open. He slipped the tape into his player. "This happened while you were out tackling Sharon May."

Lily held herself stiffly, expecting accusations from Rochelle, or perhaps a confession. Instead, the voice was Elissa Brock's.

"Hello? I'm calling for Miss Foster. I think that's her name."

And Al: "She's not here right now. Something I can help you with?"

"I just wanted to thank her. Both James and I . . . we wanted so much to thank her."

Al again, hesitantly: "I'll give her the message. Will she know what it's about?"

"Oh, yes. She's been helping us. She found James for me after all these years. I couldn't have done it myself. I hired another detective and he couldn't do it, but Miss Foster found James in Croton-on-Hudson."

"She did, huh?" Al sounded wary.

"I don't know how," Elissa went on, "but she did. He's been living there for years, ever since his divorce.

We talked for a long time on the phone. We're getting together tomorrow. I'm going out there to see his studio. He makes things out of stained glass. Little figures that he sells. We'll probably be married, the way we should have been thirty years ago. Will you tell Miss Foster for me?''

''I sure will, Mrs. Brock.''

Al shut off the tape.

''Are you mad at me?'' Lily asked.

''How did you find him?''

''The phone book. I had a hunch, from what she told me, that he was the kind who wouldn't go too far from where he started, so I looked in every phone book until I found him. It's lucky he had an unusual name. But I guess that's not very professional, is it, going by hunches.''

''You're wrong. It's very professional. A good detective always listens to his hunches. You want to be a detective, Lily?''

''I hadn't really thought about it.''

''You've been one for almost a week now, and you seem pretty good at it. You were looking for a steady job. I know you wanted something fancier than what I've got, but if you have a chance to do investigative work too, would you be willing to stay with me?''

''You mean . . . do what I'm doing now, plus investigation?''

''With a raise in pay. Maybe you could afford law school.''

Maybe she could do without law school. She would still be helping people. She had helped José—and herself.

"Could I take cases like this one? Like Elissa Brock?"

"If you insist. You handled that other one pretty well, even though it didn't work out for the parties involved."

"It's sort of a specialty," she said. "A love detective. I guess it's a branch of missing persons."

"Yes, it is," he agreed, "but with a difference. These persons have been missing for a long time." He turned to face her, his arm creeping along the back of the seat. "Are you really over that medical student?"

"It's going to take me awhile to get used to being over him," she said. "But yes, I think I am."

His hand closed over her right shoulder. Through the windshield she saw Donald and Charlene approach the building and go inside. They were holding hands and didn't see her. She smiled.

"That's the medical student?" asked Al.

"Good hunch. And my roommate."

"Well, Minnesota." His face touched her hair for just a moment. "Life is full of surprises."

"Not always," she said. "Maybe sometimes things work out the way they're supposed to."